"You tell me. What don't you want me to know? And I'm not going to give up until you tell me what—"

Suddenly, he grabbed her, pulled her tightly against him, and shut her up—by lowering his mouth firmly onto hers.

She resisted only for an instant, then threw herself into the kiss. Was this what she'd wanted all along?

One of his hands held her so firmly against him that she felt his hardness, and she pushed herself even closer. His other hand stroked first her back, then her buttocks. She moaned as it moved forward to cup one breast, tease her nipple…

"You want to know my secrets?" he rasped against her mouth.

"Then come upstairs with me, Mariah."

What could she do but comply?

Books by Linda O. Johnston

Harlequin Nocturne

*Alpha Wolf #56
Back To Life #66
*Alaskan Wolf #102

*Alpha Force

LINDA O. JOHNSTON

loves to write. More than one genre at a time? That's part of the fun. While honing her fiction, she started working in advertising and public relations, then became a lawyer...and still enjoys writing contracts. Linda's first published fiction novel appeared in *Ellery Queen's Mystery Magazine* and won a Robert L. Fish Memorial Award for "Best First Mystery Short Story of the Year." It was the beginning of her versatile fiction writing career, starting with more short stories and novellas, as well as time-travel romance and romantic suspense novels. Linda now spends most of her time creating memorable tales of paranormal romance and mystery.

As an animal aficionado, Linda enjoys writing stories in which pets and other creatures play important roles...including shape-shifters. Linda lives in the Hollywood Hills with her husband and two Cavalier King Charles spaniels. Visit her at her website, www.LindaOJohnston.com.

ALASKAN WOLF

LINDA O. JOHNSTON

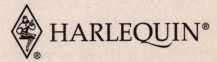

HARLEQUIN®

TORONTO • NEW YORK • LONDON
AMSTERDAM • PARIS • SYDNEY • HAMBURG
STOCKHOLM • ATHENS • TOKYO • MILAN • MADRID
PRAGUE • WARSAW • BUDAPEST • AUCKLAND

Recycling programs
for this product may
not exist in your area.

ISBN-13: 978-0-373-61849-1

ALASKAN WOLF

www.eHarlequin.com

Printed in U.S.A.

Dear Reader,

Alaskan Wolf is the second full-length novel about Alpha Force—a highly covert military unit comprised of shape-shifters. It features Lt. Patrick Worley, who is a sexy medical doctor, an Alpha Force member and—of course!—a shape-shifter, who was introduced in *Alpha Wolf* (1/09). Patrick is entrusted with a special mission to Alaska. That's where he meets magazine writer Mariah Garver.

It was great fun writing about the tension between a strong military type with amazing and inviolable secrets—like shifting into a wolf—and a curious writer who asks lots of questions and stops at nothing to learn about her specialty, wildlife. Conflict? You bet! Not to mention a romance that keeps them simmering.

I hope you enjoy it! Please come visit me at my website, www.LindaOJohnston.com and at my blog, http://KillerHobbies.blogspot.com.

Linda O. Johnston

To Alaska, where I've enjoyed some delightful journeys, including some of the best cruises ever. And to Fred, who's always there with me.

Prologue

"Destruction of the Northern Hemisphere?" Lt. Patrick Worley didn't even try to keep the disbelief from his voice. "Maybe the world?"

"Okay, could be an exaggeration," responded his superior, Major Drew Connell. His gold-colored eyes that looked so much like those of his wolf side, even when he was in human form, stared sternly at Patrick. "But it might be a real threat. One that could at least destroy parts of Alaska if it isn't stopped."

They were in Drew's office at Ft. Lukman on Maryland's Eastern Shore. It was small, but he had furnished it well with government-issue gear. Patrick just wished the chairs were more comfortable. Or maybe his discomfort today was more a result of the mission he was just offered.

One he probably couldn't refuse, even if he wanted to. Which he didn't. But he needed a better understanding of what was expected of him. "You're sure this isn't just straight global warming?" he asked. "Assuming you believe in it."

"Oh, I believe in it," Drew said. "Maybe some of this is part of a natural global cycle, maybe not. But in any case, the current annihilation of one good-sized glacier park the way it's been happening... We don't know where it could lead. There's no underground volcano, like in Iceland. If it's the result of some kind of terrorist plot, we need to know it." Drew leaned back in his seat, but his shoulders remained rigid under his standard camouflage uniform that matched Patrick's, except for the symbols of rank.

"So Alpha Force has been chosen to figure it out. Why? And why send me?" The way Patrick heard it, he was going to be pretty much on his own in Alaska, except that his aide, Sgt. Shaun Bethune, would have his back.

"Some scientists are already up there, studying and doing whatever scientists do," Drew said. "We need to know what they know, and more. To accomplish our mission, we need someone good. Smart. Someone who's been part of Alpha Force since its inception, and knows how to utilize his assets—all of them, including our brand of brew."

Patrick laughed. "Love that stuff."

"We all do," Drew agreed drily. He was the one who'd first concocted the elixir that was so important to this highly covert special ops unit. Patrick, also a medical doctor, had helped to refine it.

"In other words, a super shapeshifter who knows his stuff."

"You got it." Drew smiled for the first time. "And why Alpha Force? Because word is quietly getting out, in the right circles, that despite being relatively new, we're damn good. We can undertake assignments no other military unit could possibly hope to succeed at—not the way we do it, as fast or as well. We can approach them from more angles than anyone. So...you willing?"

"Sure am," Patrick said with no hesitation.

"Okay, then. Number one priority is to find out why those glaciers are coming apart so devastatingly and so fast. But while you're at it, you've got to maintain the secrecy of Alpha Force, and who and what we are, at all costs. Mingle with people, maintain your cover—and we've got a great one for you. Above all, study the glaciers, using everything you've got. Study everyone you meet, too—learn what they know, but without letting them get to know you and your mission. And report in to me often. Got it?"

"Yes, sir," Patrick said, giving his superior officer a mocking, yet genuine, salute.

His grin quickly faded as he turned to leave. Drew had made his point. This mission was serious.

The future of Alaska—and maybe even Alpha Force—could be riding on his success.

Chapter 1

Trying not to let her frozen breath get in her way, Mariah Garver smiled as she watched the playful huskies on the screen of her digital camera and pushed the button over and over to capture their pictures. The dogs' barks and growls filled the icy early morning air.

She panned around, from the fenced area beside her toward the house at the end of the driveway on which she stood—and stopped fast as male legs clad in jeans and boots appeared on her screen.

Lowering the camera, she looked up into the scowling face of one of the most attractive men she had ever seen—and there were plenty of great-looking men in Alaska. Sharp, handsome features were etched into a long face with a charmingly cleft chin. There was a decided sensuality to him that made her insides grow incongruously warm. But with the way he was frowning, his light brown eyes looked almost feral. In fact, she had a sense of something wild and untamed about this man.

Her sudden unease was exacerbated when he demanded harshly, "What do you want?"

"A dogsled ride." She hated how hesitant she sounded. That wasn't like her at all.

She turned off her camera and slipped it into the tote bag that she had remembered to take out of her four-wheel-drive SUV after parking at the street edge of the driveway. Squaring her shoulders beneath her all-weather vest, she strode toward the man, hearing her boots crunch over the icy surface of the driveway. Why hadn't she heard him arrive? Probably because she'd been concentrating on her photography and the noisy dogs.

She'd shot a lot of pictures of the dozens of gorgeous silvery, black-and-brown huskies cavorting playfully in the snow behind the wooden fence. They weren't wild animals. In fact, she assumed they were well domesticated, perfectly trained. But they would make a fantastic contrast with the rest of the creatures she intended to photograph around here.

"I'm Mariah Garver," she said. "I'm here to

do an article on local wildlife for *Alaskan Nature Magazine,* and I want to hire a dogsled team and musher to take me onto the ice at Great Glaciers National Park tomorrow. And you are…?"

"Wait here," he said. "I'll get Toby Dawes. He's the owner of Great Glaciers Dogsled Ranch. I only work here."

The man turned his back and strode toward the large chalet-style home behind him, at the top of the driveway.

Not exactly the way to encourage tourists and dogsledding customers, Mariah thought.

But she was nevertheless intrigued by him. He was definitely photogenic. And he somehow seemed as wild as the animals she would feature in her article.

He'd said he worked here. Maybe she could hire him to take her onto the glaciers.

The house smelled of the pungency of last night's pizza as well as the freshness of today's dog food as Patrick Worley strode inside to get his supposed boss, Toby. Patrick was steaming. Not because of the warmer temperature in the residence, and not at the woman who'd suddenly shown up on the driveway. Well, not entirely at her.

He was mostly mad at himself for overreacting, and for showing his irritation. But having someone arrive unannounced, taking pictures—for a magazine article, yet—while he was on this top-secret assignment for Alpha Force…well, it had angered him.

Justifiably, sure. He definitely didn't want anyone whose job involved curiosity—and photography—looking over his shoulder while he was going about the ordinary business of the job that was his cover.

Even someone—especially someone—as gorgeous and hot as that black-haired, curvaceous beauty, Mariah Garver. Her scent was spicy beneath her heavy clothing. Appealing, sure. But no one he needed to be near.

"Hey, Toby," Patrick yelled from the doorway. "There's a possible customer outside. She wants to talk to you."

Hearing a soft mutter from the direction of the kitchen, he headed there. Toby was at the sink, pouring warm, filtered water into a bucket of the high-calorie working-dog chow he bought by huge bagfuls for his energetic huskies. "Tell whoever it is to wait a minute," he said as Patrick walked in.

Toby Dawes was in his sixties, clearly fit and obstinately muscular. When he wasn't working his sled dogs, he was working himself.

"No need. She won't leave till she talks to you." The sexy woman writer had struck Patrick immediately as being determined. Persistent. Most likely too curious for her own good—and his. "A magazine writer,"

Patrick continued scornfully. "Taking pictures for a nature article she's writing."

That got Toby's attention. "Interesting. We could get a lot of publicity from that." He hefted the obviously heavy bucket and headed outside.

"Want me to carry that, boss?" Patrick asked.

He received a scornful glare. "I'll carry it, but you come feed our teams while I talk to the lady."

Patrick opened his mouth to object, then shut it again. He was here undercover, after all. Toby had no idea who and what he was. He had hired Patrick as a favor to a friend of his son Wes's. Wes was former Special Ops and still had a lot of military contacts, but not even he knew the truth about Patrick or his assignment. Or about Alpha Force.

Toby put the bucket down on the counter just long enough to grab his gray parka from a hook on the wall and shrug it on. Then he motioned to Patrick to follow.

The woman—Mariah—was still taking pictures. She even aimed the camera in their direction as they approached down the driveway. Patrick resisted the urge to turn in the other direction.

There were worse things than having his picture taken at this moment.

She smiled as they got closer. "Mr. Dawes? I'm really glad to meet you." She gave the same introduction as she had with Patrick.

"An article for *Alaskan Nature?* That's one of my favorite 'zines." Toby's grin lit his grizzled face as he put down the bucket he'd carried as easily as if it was filled with popcorn. "Patrick said you want to schedule a dogsled ride on the glaciers."

"That's right, tomorrow."

"Damn. I've got a meeting in Nome I can't miss, about the Iditarod. Catching a plane first thing in the morning, and won't be back till after dark." Which came earlier every day as the Alaskan winter approached.

Toby turned toward Patrick, who suddenly knew what was coming.

"How about Wes taking her?" Patrick asked. But he knew the answer. Wes was already scheduled to take a group of tourists out that day.

"Can't. But you can. Great sledding skills," he said, turning toward Mariah. "And practically a native."

If someone who'd only been here a couple of weeks could be a native, Patrick thought scornfully. He'd been trained, sure. But Toby and Wes were the best mushers around, and he'd only taken a team out on his own once.

Yet his cover required that he go along with his employer, who obviously wanted Mariah Garver's business. So, all he said was "Thanks, boss," keeping any sarcasm out of his tone.

"Looks like you hired yourself a musher," Toby said to Mariah, "long as you can meet the terms." He spouted off the cost per hour and for the extras she could choose.

Mariah didn't bat even one of those long, sexy eyelashes before saying, "That works for me." And then she aimed a gaze at Patrick that made him stand up straighter. "If Patrick is okay with it."

"Patrick is fine with it," he growled, knowing that, despite any good sense he had, he meant it.

It would mean another visit to the glaciers. That was part of what he was here for. But he would not be in the form most likely to teach him anything.

And the wariness he would have to maintain, there on the ice with this woman, would intrude on the keen observation he was capable of, even without shifting.

But, hell. He wasn't about to wait till then to visit the glaciers anyway…alone.

She had gotten her wish, Mariah thought as she drove the short distance toward the small town that was Tagoga. That hot guy—Patrick—was going to take her on her dogsled tour of the nearby glaciers.

Be careful what you wish for. The old saying flashed through her mind. Would it be a mistake to have Patrick as her tour guide? Patrick Worley— she had asked and been told his last name. She wasn't certain why she was so concerned. Maybe because Patrick appeared less than thrilled with the assignment.

Well, she still had till tomorrow morning to change her mind.

But knew she wouldn't.

Right now, it was time to return to her room at the bed-and-breakfast to get ready for the research outing scheduled for that afternoon—a boat ride into Tagoga Bay to observe and photograph Great Glaciers National Park from the water.

She smiled as she pulled into the parking lot behind her B and B.

She wouldn't worry, for now, about her upcoming dogsled tour. At the moment, she was definitely looking forward to what she would experience later today.

Twilight on Kaley Glacier.

He had visited Great Glaciers National Park half a dozen times since coming to Alaska. So far, he had seen, heard, smelled nothing beyond the ordinary. The cold had a tight, biting scent. The few birds that flew quickly by overhead smelled comfortably warmer. The brine of the waters below was tangy, hinting of fish.

The frigid cold clutching the bareness of the

toughened skin of his feet was almost unbearable. At least his thick pelt of fur kept the rest of him warm.

It was early nightfall, nearly, but not quite, dark. He would remain here, opening his senses further, waiting for anything to happen this evening. Another step in the decimation of Great Glaciers National Park?

Mounds of snow and crags of ice on this glacier provided little cover from the whistling wind. He continued to patrol, watching, waiting.

And then—he inhaled deeply. The distant scent was suddenly hot. Fiery...here? Almost metallic, yet underlain with the ozone of melting ice.

The sound was odd, like the shrill, pulsing cries of orcas. Yet he scented no killer whales in the water below. Were some there nevertheless, trumpeting fear because they, too, smelled that odor? Knew what it meant?

A sharp, abrupt explosive noise. And then—

What was the low rumbling beneath the orcas' calls? It grew louder. Sharp. Angry. A huge roar that made the ice tremble beneath his feet.

No! The surface wasn't merely trembling. It was separating. The glacier was calving, right where he stood.

He pivoted, ran inland on all fours. Heard the

cracking behind him. Felt the vibration of the surface below his paws. Would he be tossed into the frigid waters by separating ice?

An enormous splash resounded behind him. The movement lessened. He turned...and watched.

Most of the ice that was once behind him was gone. Warily, he approached the new craggy edge. He saw the separated mass slide beneath the gray-blue surface of the bay below, no longer part of the glacier but an ice floe.

He waited in wonder. This was what he was here to investigate, but he had no answers. If something beyond nature caused this, he still had no clue. Except, perhaps, what he had heard and smelled. But what did that mean?

He heard an engine. He looked into the sea beneath the reddening twilight sky and saw a boat approach. The new ice floe was invisible beneath the water, and would harm anything in its path as it surfaced. But though the boat was pitching, it did not appear to be in danger.

Not that he could help them.

He saw the new iceberg leap from the water, then settle back in the roiling bay.

Then he turned and paced the newly formed edge of the glacier, a lone wolf prowling the ice.

And watching that boat.

* * *

In the orange glow reflected from the gleaming sunset, Mariah stared at the remainder of the glacier as the huge new iceberg erupted from the water and sank again. Quickly, she darted her eyes to her camera screen and back to the incredible sight.

With her other hand, she clutched the rail at the edge of the fishing boat's deck. Never mind that the hood on her navy Windbreaker had blown off and left her hair flying in the rush of air caused by the boat's heaving, her ears suddenly freezing. She had to watch. Record it all in movie mode. And keep from plunging overboard.

She'd thought, when she'd hired this fishing boat and its captain, that the craft was substantial enough to do well in all but the worst weather.

But the weather was fine. It was the water that heaved, tossing the boat as perilously as if it was a toy in a wading pool being slapped by a gleeful child.

No matter. Despite her shivering from uneasiness and cold, she had to record every moment. She'd be able to cull some still pictures when she was done, and upload them onto her computer. Use them for the article she was researching.

The ice floe settled into the water, calm now, as if it hadn't just torn away from the mass above. Then, a few dead fish floated to the surface near the ice. Poor things, Mariah thought.

A short distance away, Mariah saw a pair of sea otters floating on top of the water, not in the path of the ice floe, fortunately. They didn't appear particularly impressed by the calving as they swam slowly in circles. Mariah snapped some pictures for her article. The poor creatures appeared sluggish. Were they in shock? At least they were alive.

Mariah looked back at the jagged glacier surface— and thought she saw a movement at the top. An animal? Unlikely, but she aimed her camera in that direction.

Using the strongest telephoto setting, she saw clearly in the camera screen that it was a wolf, its deep gray coat silhouetted against the whiteness of the glacial surface. It was pacing uneasily. Majestic. Gorgeous. She filmed it despite knowing that the creature was too far away to obtain a really good photo. Was it looking at the boat? Her?

What an odd impression!

Maybe she would see the wolf again, closer, when she took her dogsled ride onto the glaciers with Patrick Worley.

Patrick. His face suddenly filled her mind, as if he were somewhere around here.

She almost laughed out loud at the ridiculous turns her imagination had taken.

"Getting what you need?" Nathan Kugan's voice startled her.

The captain had come from the bridge of his boat to join her on deck. Half a foot taller than her five-two, he was a local, of Aleutian descent, and the crispness of the fall air whipping across the deck apparently didn't bother him. He wore only a light sweater over his jeans and boots.

"I think so," Mariah said, glad for the interruption to her absurd thoughts. She lowered her camera at his approach. "I'm recording what's happening, at least. Now I need to look more into what's causing it."

"Did you get the whales?"

She frowned. "I haven't seen any whales. The only living sea animals I glimpsed were those otters." She pointed.

His turn to frown, deepening the creases in his weathered face. Mariah had guessed him to be mid-fifties, but he looked ageless and could have been a lot older. "I had my acoustical equipment turned on—sonar, and the microphones I use to listen for fish. Before the noise from the glacier calving, I heard what sounded like orca calls. You didn't see any?"

Odd term, calving. She knew it, of course, since she had lived in Alaska for three years now, but she would have to explain it in her article for nonlocal readers. It described the tearing away of huge chunks of ice from the edges of glaciers nearest the water. As if the ice fields were happily producing bouncing, enormous babies which, if large enough, were icebergs.

"No. I wish I had." She took her camera and panned the bay, still using her telephoto setting in case something appeared in the distance. The sun had slid beneath the horizon, and the remaining light of day was following in its wake. Even in the growing darkness, the black-and-white irregular stripes found on killer whales would still be visible, giving away their location.

But she saw no orcas anywhere.

Nathan squinted and looked at the darkening water. "Strange. They sounded close. Should be surfacing by now to breathe."

"Maybe they were heading out the mouth of the bay," Mariah suggested.

"Could be. They're smart animals. They might have sensed the calving would occur and warned one another to leave."

Mariah knew enough about orcas, members of the dolphin family, to accept their intelligence. What Nathan suggested was within the realm of possibility.

"You saw the glacier calving, didn't you?" she asked. The water was settling down, and Mariah let go of the ship's rail, though she still leaned against it for balance.

"Yes. It's maybe the eighth major calving I've seen in Tagoga Bay this week. Too many."

"I'm surprised none of the scientists visiting the town are here now."

Government, university and even private studies were being conducted in this area, in an attempt to determine the cause of the growing destruction of these glaciers. Was global warming acting this fast in Alaska?

That wasn't Mariah's focus, of course. The area's nature, including its wildlife, was what she would write about. Like the sluggish otters. And that solitary wolf, obviously upset by the glacier's tearing. But if she learned something else of interest, she would include it, too.

She thought again, incongruously, of Patrick Worley. What might he have thought about this particular glacier's calving? And why had she gotten that absurd sense of his presence?

"Thing is," Nathan said, staring off toward the glacier field, "there's always calving. Small pieces, sometimes larger ones, every day. Cruise ships even entertain their passengers on occasion by blowing their whistles and getting ice to break off. But I've never seen anything on this scale before."

"Any idea why?" Mariah asked.

He shook his head. "Nope. It's sad, though. You ready to go back to town?"

"Yes, thanks." She had plans for the evening. She'd scheduled an interview that night with some of the visiting scientists conducting research.

Time to focus even more on her article.

And get good-looking dogsled mushers out of her mind until it was time for her ride.

Chapter 2

Fiske's Hangout was an amazing place. Mariah had thought so when she had first come in here the previous afternoon. This evening, it still made one heck of an impression. It also had a convenience store and post office attached—truly an all-purpose place to serve this small town.

She stood in the crowded bar/restaurant doorway now, hearing the roar of voices, looking for people she recognized—like anyone she had seen at the Great Glaciers Dogsled Ranch. Finding no one she had met there, she felt a small pang of disappointment, which was ludicrous. Her sled dog ride would take place tomorrow. She could get her fix of seeing Patrick Worley then.

She nearly laughed at herself—especially after that silly notion of his presence somewhere nearby while she was on the boat, watching the glacier, the otters and the wolf.

She stepped farther in. It was time for her meeting with Dr. Emil Charteris, a noted glaciologist who had studied the melting of the ice in Antarctica and Greenland, and who now had a federal grant to study the glacial changes here. With him was his research team: his son-in-law, Jeremy Thaxton, a zoologist, and his daughter, Carrie Thaxton, a computer expert. Mariah was curious to hear Dr. Charteris's ideas of why the glaciers in this area were falling apart so quickly, but she particularly wanted to focus on Jeremy Thaxton's perspective of the possible climate change's effect on local wildlife.

Fiske's Hangout was the best location to meet anyone in this town. Mariah especially liked the charming wooden bar in its middle—a tall, hand-carved box, with winged maidens resembling figureheads at its corners. Gargoyles and pixies peered from center shelves holding bottles and glasses. Supposedly, the bar's first owner got bored during his first dark, cold Alaskan winter and spent otherwise idle hours carving this masterpiece. True or not, the place was incredible.

As she continued scanning the crowd, she recognized the people she sought from their online photos. Unlike most Hangout patrons, Dr. Charteris and his family members did not mill around the bar. Instead, they sat at one of the white spruce tables scattered haphazardly along the rest of the wood floor that was all but obscured by peanut shells. Mariah crunched her way toward them.

"Hello, Dr. Charteris." She extended her hand. "I'm Mariah Garver."

"Ah, yes. The nature writer." His rising apparently signaled his daughter and son-in-law, who also stood. Emil Charteris was over six feet tall, and there was a well-worn cragginess to his long face. His deep brown hair was silvered at the temples. "Please join us," he said, "and tell us more about the article you're researching. I'm not sure we can add much exciting information, but we'll certainly try."

"I'd appreciate it." Mariah smiled.

Carrie and Jeremy also introduced themselves as they resumed their seats. Carrie, known as a computer whiz and statistician, was willowy and tall, like her dad—attractive, and maybe a few years older than Mariah's age of thirty-one. Her snug red sweater hugged her slight bustline, making Mariah aware of her own, more substantial curviness.

Jeremy was about his wife's height, and he wore glasses. His forehead puckered in what appeared to be perpetual concern. Mariah particularly focused on him, since he would have the most information pertinent to her article.

Almost immediately, a short, stocky woman wearing a heavy, patterned sweater and bucktoothed grin stood beside them, a pad and pen poised in her hands. "Okay, I know the professor, Carrie and Jeremy," she said. "And you are…?" She looked expectantly at Mariah, who gave her name. "Case you can't guess," the woman said, "I'm Thea Fiske. Fiske's Hangout is mine. You're welcome as long as you eat, drink and cause no trouble." She winked beneath the crown of silvery braids that wrapped her head. "Got it?"

"Uh-oh." Mariah pretended concern. "Okay, I'll have a mug of hot, spiked cider and…what would you recommend to eat?"

The choices unsurprisingly turned out to be mostly Alaskan style—primarily salmon and other seafood, and even moose steak. Mariah, who had fallen hard for Alaskan fare when she moved to Juneau a few years earlier, opted for the salmon, as did most of the others.

As soon as Thea left, Mariah explained that her article would be about local wildlife, especially on and around the glaciers, focusing on whether changes to the ice fields affected the animals. Then she started asking questions. "How long have you been in Tagoga?" She looked expectantly at Emil, to her right.

The bar/restaurant's acoustics were surprisingly good. Despite the low roar of conversations from the large crowd and the background music played with zeal by a piano player in one corner, Mariah had no trouble hearing his response. She had, with consent, put a recorder on the table, but it wasn't the latest technology and she feared it wouldn't pick up everything.

"About six weeks. Jeremy and Carrie joined me a month ago." He waited while Thea plunked bread in front of them, then explained what he hoped to accomplish: collect as much data as he could on the extent of global warming's effects in this area, and on whether something else could be causing the extreme acceleration of the melting of the glaciers.

Definitely interesting, but Mariah wanted to learn more about effects than causes.

She was pleased when Jeremy dived into the conversation. "I've barely scratched the surface of researching native wildlife at Great Glaciers, and whether the glacial changes affect various species." He chewed thoughtfully on a piece of bread. "But I'll be looking into it."

"I was at the park earlier this evening on a boat," Mariah said, "and saw a glacier calving. A huge piece broke off, and the captain says that's been happening a lot more than normal even just this week. He described some orca sounds, though I didn't hear them. But I saw a couple of otters in the bay, and a wolf on the remaining part of the glacier."

The scientists had been there, too, earlier that day, and hadn't seen that particular calving of Kaley Glacier, but they all compared notes. Mariah showed the photos on her digital camera, including the otters and wolf, and Jeremy expressed particular interest in following up on the creatures.

Learning that Carrie was compiling statistics on the calving and related issues, Mariah promised to provide any information she gathered, and was delighted when Carrie agreed to give her copies of her spreadsheets.

Mariah had just taken a sip of cider when the piano music in the corner stopped suddenly. So did most of the talking in the bar. Everyone seemed to glance in one direction—toward the door.

So did Mariah.

Just inside stood three tall men. Mariah didn't understand why there'd been such a reaction in Fiske's Hangout. They certainly weren't the only people to have entered the place since she had arrived.

And surely she was the only one around here whose heart momentarily stopped on seeing Patrick Worley, the one in the middle.

They all wore heavy jackets, but his was unzipped,

revealing a deep blue sweater. His eyes played around the room…and stopped when he saw her.

He didn't smile. In fact, he looked a little… displeased to see her. She wondered why.

Well, better that way. She seemed to be reacting all out of proportion to this man who clearly wanted nothing to do with her. She wasn't a fool. She needed his dogsledding services, and once he had fulfilled that purpose she would never need to see, or think about, him again.

A few loud chords sounded from the piano, and the musician began playing the old, appropriate song, "North to Alaska," singing loudly. A few patrons joined in as the place seemed to relax, and people returned to their drinks. Mariah's tablemates resumed eating their dinners.

"You want another of those?" Thea hovered over their table as she did so often that evening. She pointed toward Mariah's almost empty glass of cider.

"Sure," she said. "Thanks." Her gaze automatically returned to the newcomers, who had found bar stools near the table where Mariah sat with her interviewees.

Thea leaned down and said conspiratorially in Mariah's ear, "Real hotties, aren't they?" She shrugged a hefty shoulder in the direction of the new arrivals. "They all work at the Great Glaciers Dogsled Ranch."

Not surprisingly, Mariah thought, although she hadn't met the other two.

"Why did everything go quiet when they came in?" she couldn't help asking.

Thea looked puzzled. "It did, didn't it?" Her round face scrunched into a pensive frown. "Coincidence, probably. No one planned it. But…" Her voice tapered off.

"But what?" Mariah asked curiously.

"It's the kind of thing that my mother used to say meant that even if no one realized it, they all heard an angel whispering and had to stop talking to listen… an angel of death."

Mariah laughed uneasily. "My grandfather was superstitious and came up with things like that for nearly every occasion."

"Don't just laugh it off," Thea warned. She walked away and, watching her, Mariah found herself looking toward the bar.

Patrick stared right back.

And despite how far he was from her, and the fact the piano music blared again over loud conversations, she had the oddest sense that he had heard every word.

"Is that the lady you were talking about?" Shaun asked Patrick as they stood in the crowd at the bar.

Sgt. Shaun Bethune of the U.S. military's very special Ops unit Alpha Force, was assigned as chief aide to Lt. Patrick Worley, and both held jobs at the Great Glaciers Dogsled Ranch as part of their cover.

"Yeah, I saw her at the ranch talking to my dad and Patrick," Wes Dawes said. "Too bad I'm not available to take her out for that ride she booked, you lucky SOB. She's hot." Wes, a former marine, once had top security clearance. He didn't know exactly what Patrick and Shaun's mission was but was aware they were performing a covert operation for the military and was happy to assist by providing jobs for the two men.

Patrick bristled at Wes's description of Mariah. Sure, she was hot. He just didn't like to hear Wes say so, though he didn't know why he gave a damn. "Yeah, sure, I'm lucky. I'm taking her out on the glaciers. That's all."

It wasn't all, though. She had been on that fishing boat in the bay, Patrick was certain. He had sensed her presence, even from that distance. And the people she was talking to now were of real interest to Patrick in fulfilling his assignment here. He hadn't yet found a way to get together with them and initiate a conversation. Until, perhaps, tonight.

And right now, he could continue eavesdropping on their answers to her questions about the glaciers.

"Your bad luck," Shaun said. "So, bro, you're

drinking beer tonight?" He elbowed Patrick gently in the ribs as they reached the bar. "I thought you were on the wagon." Of course, Shaun knew what was what. A few hours earlier, with Shaun keeping watch nearby, Patrick had drunk some of the highly classified and extremely potent Alpha Force elixir.

Combined with an artificial light he traveled with, the elixir allowed beings like him to shapeshift at will, not just under the full moon. Plus, it ensured that he kept all his human awareness and thinking abilities. Invaluable.

It had all but worn off now, but major alcohol consumption so close to that elixir wasn't a great idea.

Still, a bottle of beer could be nursed for a while. And part of Patrick's cover was to act like the itinerant drifter he was supposed to be. Someone in his position wouldn't hesitate to have a beer. Or two.

And maybe get a little outspoken as a result…

"Aw, leave him alone," Wes said. He had no knowledge of what Patrick really was. To him, Patrick was to be treated mostly as another hired musher, despite being on an undisclosed military mission.

Major Drew Connell had been right. Patrick did have a great cover here. He liked working for Wes and his dad, Toby. Even more, he enjoyed working with dogs and had brought his own—well, his cover dog, since theoretically Duke, one hell of a great shepherd-wolfhound mix and trained as a scent and security dog, belonged to Uncle Sam.

Once they had their beers, the guys elbowed their way from the bar again, Shaun in the lead. He was a good guy whose hobby happened to be wrestling, and he had the beefy, muscular physique of a winner.

They stopped at the edge of the crowd. Patrick took a stiff drink while pretending to look for an empty table—a useless task in this mass of people.

Instead, he was still listening. His senses, while he was in human form, were nearly as good as while he was wolfen, especially this soon after he'd changed. Despite the clinkety-clink piano music, the irritating yet soft sound of people stepping on peanut shells, the off-key singing, all the other background noise, he heard everything being said at Mariah's table. Nothing especially useful yet, but he would continue to listen. And to keep an eye on her. Not a hardship.

It grew easier to hear when the music stopped. He glanced toward the piano and saw that the other woman from the table, Carrie Thaxton—daughter of the man who was Patrick's objective tonight— approached the musician, handed him a tip. "Play 'Jingle Bells' for me," she said.

"Gladly." Soon an enthusiastic rendition of that song reverberated throughout the bar, sung not only by the pianist but by patrons in various stages of inebriation.

Great. This way, Patrick wouldn't learn anything much since conversations wouldn't flourish.

But he had an idea. As soon as the song was over, he picked up his beer bottle and went to the pianist himself.

The piano was an upright that had seen better days. Its light wood was scuffed. But it sounded all right. "Hey, your music is great," he said to the guy who sat there. "I'm Patrick Worley. I'm new around here, work at the Great Glaciers Dogsled Ranch. What's your name?"

"Andy Lemon." He was pale, maybe late forties, and obviously pretty nearsighted, judging by the thickness of his small, black-framed glasses.

"You been playing here long?" Patrick asked.

"Not very, but it's a great place."

"Sure is. And right now, Andy Lemon, I'd love for you to play some nice, soft, romantic songs for the next ten minutes." Patrick whipped out a twenty-dollar bill in emphasis. "There's a woman here I really want to get to know, and I'd like to put her in the mood to get to know me, too. Okay?" He nudged the guy, who grinned, revealing a set of yellow teeth.

"You got it, Patrick. Good luck." He played a few melodic riffs, then began a schmaltzy, low instrumental rendition of Elvis's "Can't Help Falling in Love."

Motioning for Shaun and Wes to follow, Patrick approached the table where Mariah Garver sat with Emil Charteris and his family members.

"Hi," he said, looking down at her. "Mind if we join you?"

"There's not a lot of room," she said, "but if you can find some chairs…" She looked around at the others she sat with, and none, fortunately, objected.

Shaun and Wes had already fulfilled the assignment she'd given, although Patrick wouldn't ask how they'd managed to liberate three chairs so quickly. Soon, they were all seated at the table.

"This is Patrick Worley," Mariah said, introducing him to the others. Lord, did she make him feel warm and uncomfortable in his sweater and jeans, just by looking at him with her luscious, luminous—and incisive—blue eyes. "Dr. Emil Charteris and the Thaxtons. I'm interviewing them for the article for *Alaskan Nature Magazine* I'm writing—the one I also need the dogsled ride for as research." She explained the scientific backgrounds of the three scientists.

Patrick in turn, introduced Mariah and her friends to his dogsled ranch companions.

"So what's the scoop about the glaciers?" Patrick hoped his tone sounded entirely conversational. His ploy to finally talk to Emil Charteris seemed to be working, even though these people generally kept to themselves. "We got here only recently, Shaun and I, but from what we heard we may not be able to take people out on dogsled rides much longer, the way they're melting."

"Wish I knew what to tell you," Emil Charteris said. "But that's part of why we're here—to see if there's something even worse going on than global warming, which is usually bad enough."

"I'm most concerned about how this trend may harm the wildlife around here," Mariah said. "That's Jeremy's expertise."

Patrick's interest was focused almost entirely on the glaciers, not the wildlife. Still, he found himself listening to Mariah's melodic voice, inhaling the surprisingly spicy scent she wore considering her down-to-earth demeanor.... Hell, he had to stop this. He had come over here hoping for information helpful to his investigation, and she was turning the discussion in a different direction.

"Do you know, Mariah said she saw a wolf on top of Kaley Glacier right after it calved?" interjected Carrie Thaxton. She gave Patrick the impression she didn't like anyone else to be the center of attention, especially another woman. "I think that's wild, don't you?"

"Wolves do tend to be wild," her husband said drily. The look Jeremy gave his wife was both condescending and caring. His scent suggested he used a lot of antiseptic hand cleanser.

"That's not what I mean and you know it." She gave him a gentle shove.

"One interesting thing about the wolf was that it appeared to be alone," Mariah said. Patrick had the impression she was trying to keep the peace at the table as much as get the discussion back on the topic of her interest.

"They're usually pack animals, of course," Jeremy confirmed, "but you only glimpsed that one. Could be the rest of his pack was somewhere you couldn't see from the water."

"We'll check that out tomorrow when we take the dogsled onto the glaciers, right, Patrick?" Mariah asked.

She sounded so enthusiastic that he could do little but agree with her. "Absolutely," he said.

Mariah wasn't sure how much she should look forward to her outing with Patrick Worley. He would be a real distraction to her research, if she weren't careful. He was tall. Broad shouldered beneath his blue sweater—good thing he'd taken off the jacket that obscured that delicious view. Sharp, handsome features etched into a long face.

And why had he sat down here? She'd had the initial impression he wasn't happy to see her.

"How's your salmon?" Thea Fiske had come over to the table, bringing a basket of fresh rolls.

"A little dry," Carrie said. "Otherwise, it's okay."

"Not just okay," Mariah contradicted after noticing Thea's hurt look. "Mine's delicious."

Their hostess gave her a broad grin, then leaned down and whispered in her ear, "Hey, those mushers—they're good company on cold Alaskan nights, honey. And that new guy, Patrick—looks like he wants to get to know you. I can tell."

Mariah felt herself flush. "I doubt it," she responded softly right back. "And if so, he can hope all he wants."

Thea just straightened and winked. Which only made Mariah feel all the more uncomfortable— especially since, when she glanced again at Patrick, he was watching her. She had the unnerving impression that he knew exactly what Thea had said.

But his attention wasn't entirely focused on her. Unlike his two friends, engaged in a muted conversation together, Patrick seemed interested in her companions at the table.

"So tell me your theory so far on the melting of the glaciers, Emil," he said to Dr. Charteris, who had just taken the last bite of his meal.

"Still working on it," he said.

"Of course," Patrick agreed. "But—"

"We've got a big day tomorrow, Dad," Carrie Thaxton interrupted. "You finished eating? We'd better run."

Her husband was still chewing, but Emil agreed with Carrie and motioned toward Thea for the check.

"Oh, no, this is on me," Mariah said. "I appreciate your talking to me, and hope I can schedule another interview with you soon—maybe after I've gotten my dogsled ride on the glaciers and had a chance to observe any wildlife on the ice. Okay?"

"Of course," Emil said. "Anytime."

Mariah had the impression that his daughter and son-in-law were less enthused by the idea, but neither objected. Of course, she'd have to see if they'd actually agree on a time and place for a follow-up interview.

Thea Fiske came over with the bill, and Mariah pulled out her credit card.

"See you soon," Mariah said as Emil and the others left. She turned back toward those remaining at the table to find Patrick watching Emil and his family wend their way through the crowd. There was an expression on Patrick's face that she couldn't quite understand—as if he was angry at their departure.

He must have sensed she was watching. He turned back toward her and smiled. "Dessert? Something else to drink? My treat."

She was getting tired. And a bit uncomfortable after Thea's observation and her own much too substantial interest in Patrick. He was not her type—no matter how sexy he was. After past bad experience, she had no interest in men who weren't focused on genuine careers. Stable.

"No, thanks," she said. "I'll be leaving now, too. See you around, everyone. And, Patrick, I'll definitely see you at the dogsled ranch tomorrow for my ride."

"I was just thinking of heading out, too," he said. "I'll walk with you."

Not a good idea, Mariah thought, but didn't immediately come up with a tactful way to tell him to get lost.

She didn't need to be tactful with him, she realized. Even so, she didn't want to tell him to stay away—not if she wanted him to remain available for her dogsled ride.

"You up for another beer?" Shaun said to Wes. He nodded, and they stood. She wasn't even going to get the comfort of having a crowd come along as she left.

She rose. "Why don't you join your friends?" she asked Patrick.

"I've had enough." He helped her maneuver through the crowd to the door, and walked outside with her.

In a moment, he looked down at her in the light from the streetlamp. The shivers that swept up and down her spine like the fingers of the musician on the piano inside were not entirely from the chilliness of the night air.

Something in Patrick's light brown eyes looked… well, feral—but most definitely sensual.

"Where are you staying?" he asked.

"Oh, just down the street, but no need to—"

"I'll walk you there," he said.

Opening her mouth to protest, she was amazed to hear herself say, "I'd enjoy the company."

Chapter 3

The sounds of bar conversation accented by piano music receded quickly into the background as Mariah walked beside Patrick along the sidewalk toward her B and B. In the chilly late fall air in this small Alaskan town, there were few night sounds—a car or two driving by, the buzz from other gathering places—and her concentration was engulfed by Patrick's presence.

Despite her heavy jacket and boots lined in faux fur, she felt the cold and wondered briefly what it would be like to walk closer to Patrick, sharing his warmth.

And nearly laughed aloud at her foolishness.

Especially since the silence between them seemed to expand exponentially. Why had she agreed to allow him to accompany her at all?

"So you live in Juneau?" he asked, obviously attempting to relieve the strained discomfort.

"That's right." For the same reason, she kept talking. She briefly explained her background: growing up in Chicago, a degree from Purdue in Natural Resources and Environmental Science. A love of wildlife enhanced by working summers at a state park.

No need to go into more personal history, like coming from a wealthy family that lost it all by risky—and worse—investments in bad economic times. Or how that affected a recent relationship she had briefly and painfully thought to be true love.

Nor would she mention her last job writing incisive articles on people, not animals—sometimes amounting to near sensationalism. That was in the past.

"A job as a staff writer for *Alaskan Nature Magazine* is a dream come true," she finished. "There's no place else in the U.S. with so much unique wildlife in an unexplored and pristine habitat. And how about you? How did you decide to work on a dogsled ranch?"

His turn to break the silence.

"I needed a different direction for my life, and Alaska seemed like a good place to start."

She waited for him to continue, but he didn't. All she heard was the sound of their footsteps crunching on the salt strewn on the sidewalks to melt ice. Their way along the town's main street, Tagoga Avenue, was illuminated by the occasional streetlight as they walked by closed businesses that sold everything from the heavy clothing needed for the upcoming winter, to hunting gear—which made Mariah shiver. She was not a vegetarian, but her love of wildlife caused her to cringe at the thought of killing the beautiful and majestic creatures in Alaska's wilderness. As a resident of this glorious state, though, she had come to terms with it, as long as hunting was done for food and not simply for trophies or fur. And the culling of predatory animals like wolves to protect game, like caribou—not something she could buy into.

The silence grew uncomfortable again. Mariah wondered why Patrick wasn't saying more about his background, especially after all she had spewed out to him about herself.

Was he hiding something?

She was a magazine writer, not an investigative journalist—or even a paparazzo—now, but she still enjoyed tossing controversy into her stories where appropriate. She reveled in her curiosity and cultivated the knack of prying out of people details of their interest in, and treatment of, wildlife—good and bad.

She wasn't about to allow Patrick to get away with his reticence.

"So what did you do before that required a change?" she asked, trying to keep her tone light.

"This and that." Hearing amusement in his voice, she looked up to find him smiling at her. And what a smile. Despite the wary ruefulness she read in it and his body language—hands stuffed stiffly into the pockets at the side of his rustic jacket—the guy was gorgeous. Sexy.

Intriguing.

She wanted to know more. A lot more.

But they had just turned the corner onto Kaley Street. Her B and B was on this block, and Patrick apparently knew that. He picked up his pace.

"What *this* and what *that?*" She tried to make her demand sound like idle chitchat, but she wanted answers.

"Isn't this where you're staying?" Patrick had stopped in front of a three-story redbrick building that was, in fact, Mariah's B and B—Inez's Inn. A bright yellow light illuminated the large, closed white door with a stylized, smiling moose face hung at the top.

"Well, yes," she said. "But I'd really like to know—"

Before she could insist any further, he leaned down. Grasped her arms.

And lowered his face toward hers.

Quite unexpectedly, the thought that crossed her mind earlier, sharing his warmth, turned into reality as he melded his body against hers. He covered her lips with his, expertly insisting on her kissing him back. His kiss was fiery in the briskness of the surrounding air, his tongue searching, suggestive of even more sensual delights.

She shivered, leaning against him, her body suddenly and sensitively primed for more.

A sound of voices erupted from inside the building, and in moments Patrick stood several feet away. He looked bemused, then another expression—anger?—washed over his face.

He looked into her eyes almost challengingly. "See you tomorrow, Ms. Garver."

He strode away into the night as the door opened behind her.

It was ten o'clock the next morning. The time Mariah Garver was scheduled to appear at Great Glaciers Dogsled Ranch.

Toby Dawes was off to his meeting in Nome. Wes was out with the tour group. Most of the ranch's other employees were also already hosting tourists, except for Shaun.

Patrick stood inside the main house, keeping an eye on the antics of the dogs in the fenced-in area below, including his own dog, Duke.

Mostly, he watched the driveway, certain Mariah wouldn't appear. He hoped fervently that he'd chased her away with that kiss last night, not that it had been his intention at the time.

At this point, he wasn't sure what he had intended. Oh, sure, he'd wanted to keep her from asking more questions about his background. He had a cover story, of course—one that Shaun and he had developed, with input from others on Alpha Force. Wes Dawes, with his military background, knew one version— some unspecified covert assignment. But the rest of the world was to be fed quite a different story.

One Patrick feared that inquisitive Mariah might see right through.

But, hell, he couldn't change it. It was the background Toby knew. So did other ranch employees. If necessary, he would feed it to Mariah, too, then shut up about it. Let her wonder without being sure.

Better yet, he wouldn't have to see her again, ever, if she didn't come for her sled ride. Although… some part of him didn't like that idea, either. He was attracted to her. Had been even before that spontaneous kiss. And after? Hell, he wanted her. All of her. In bed, where they would create their own uninhibited heat in a fiery bout of mind-blowing sex, and—

Dream on, Worley. That was one bad idea. First and foremost, Mariah was a nosy writer. One who was into wildlife. If she ever learned just how close he was to nature, his secret would be out. Worse, so would Alpha Force's secrets.

That could not happen.

Patrick glanced at the waterproof watch on his wrist. Ten-fifteen. Good. Maybe she actually had decided to stay far away. He'd wait another couple of minutes, then go back to the building where the ranch hands had tiny apartments, check on Shaun and his online research, and—

An SUV pulled in at the bottom of the driveway. The one he had seen here yesterday. Mariah's.

Damn. Time for the show to begin.

But first he'd have to erase the big, inappropriate grin from his face.

So far, the outing hadn't been too awkward, Mariah thought with relief as Patrick showed her how to sit on the sled to which he had already harnessed the team of dogs—nine, all unique-looking Alaskan huskies, which he had explained were a combination of diverse breeds, chosen more for their intelligence and performance than their bloodlines.

After a restless night, with that kiss replaying over

and over in her mind, she had considered postponing her ride to another day—like the fifteenth of never.

But she was here to research her article. She could ignore her discomfort in Patrick's company to accomplish what she needed to. She hoped.

Besides, she had a strong suspicion that the kiss was an attempt by Patrick to get her to stop asking questions. Which meant he had something to hide. If so, she was even more intrigued to learn all she could about him.

Now, they were in a small, ice-covered area between the main road and the glacier park. They had driven here in a sturdy van with carpeting in the rear for the dogs, the ride crammed full of instructions from Patrick on what to expect on the sled and how to stay safe.

No time to ask him more about himself.

In a short while, they were ready to mush off. "Let's go!" he called to the huskies. They all rose, including the lead dog, Mac—short for McKinley, Patrick told her—and soon ran out over the crushed ice surface of the glacier, towing the sled.

It was exhilarating! The frigid air pelted Mariah's cheeks, and she was glad she had bundled up with a knit hat and scarf as well as her warm jacket, slacks and boots.

She couldn't easily turn to ask Patrick questions, but they'd also discussed her expectations on the ride here. When they spotted a bald eagle circling the first glacier on their expedition, he signaled to the dogs to slow down by calling "Whoa" and pulling back on the tug line attached to the gang line hooked to each dog's harness. She grabbed her camera from the bag slung over her shoulder, hoping to shoot the photos she wanted without freezing her hands, since she had to remove her thick gloves.

She wished she had come here before the changes to the glaciers, to be able to compare then and now herself. That would make her article more intriguing than simply focusing on the animals she saw on this trip. She hoped to at least get insight, from Jeremy Thaxton or other biologists studying the area, on the kinds and numbers of creatures who'd previously been plentiful here, and whether the numbers seemed to have changed.

And how many wolves there were.

The glacier's surface was irregular—eroded, abounding with ice mounds and cracks. Eventually, near the far edge of the ice that created a cliff overlooking the bay, they stopped. Patrick helped Mariah off the sled and directed the dogs to lie down on the snowy crust.

"Won't they freeze there?" Mariah asked, concerned about the work animals.

"They're used to it. And they'll huddle together if it becomes too difficult."

"Like a nine-dog day," Mariah quipped. She knew that the old vocal group Three Dog Night had taken its name from the way people who spent a lot of time in climates like this described the degree of a night's coldness by the number of dogs they needed to snuggle with to stay warm.

"Exactly." His look at her seemed—well, not just kind, but almost amused. Caring. Where did that come from?

It warmed her from the inside. And made her wonder whether one of those kisses from last night might make her even warmer way out here.

They were soon off again. In the distance, on an ice-covered mountainside, Mariah made out a pair of Dall sheep. She shot a lot of photos, though the majestic animals were too far away to see well.

At one point, a small flock of black-legged kittiwakes flew by. The gull-like birds cried out shrilly as they passed. Again, Mariah took pictures. They also saw cormorants, but no puffins, although Mariah would have loved to have viewed some.

Maybe she would come back here on her own someday. She loved cross-country skiing and had become even better at it since moving to Alaska. The glaciers would make a wonderful landscape for skiing.

Patrick and she spent nearly three hours visiting quite a few glaciers in Great Glaciers National Park.

They ran into no one on the ice, not even any of the scientists researching what was happening here. They also observed no calving that day, a good thing for their safety but not necessarily good for the research Mariah hoped to accomplish.

Among the glaciers they visited was Kaley Glacier, the one Mariah had observed calving yesterday. When they stopped near its edge, she got out and looked in all directions, including the surface of the ice—hoping to see paw prints. But there were none.

"See any signs of a wolf around here?" she asked Patrick.

"No," he responded curtly, staring into the distance as if he was looking for…what? The wolf? Somehow, Mariah didn't think so.

"I saw one up here," she insisted. "There was probably a lot of wind last night, and maybe some snow fell, so I'm not surprised I didn't see any tracks, but I'd really love to find a sign, anything I can photograph, to use in my article."

"I don't see anything," he insisted. Mariah wondered at his adamant tone, as if he wanted to deny everything she said.

"But I—"

"Look. There are some sea otters, down in the water." He pointed to a spot in the bay way below them. The creatures were tiny, but Mariah's camera had an excellent telephoto lens, and she got some good photos of them reclining on their backs in the water eating whatever seafood they had caught. They seemed more energetic than the ones she had seen yesterday.

But despite Patrick's obvious attempt to help her garner wildlife photos, she wondered about his earlier attitude about the wolf she'd seen.

Eventually, they returned to the van. Patrick unlocked it and let Mariah into the cab, while he unhitched the dogs and ordered them inside. Soon, the sled had also been loaded.

"That was fantastic!" Mariah exclaimed as Patrick joined her in the truck. "I loved it."

"I'm glad." He actually sounded as if he meant it. "It was a good day for an outing like this—no precipitation."

"I hope it's just as good next time." She watched for his reaction. His relaxed features hardened but he said nothing. "I'd love to go again in a few days. I only scratched the surface of investigating local wildlife and any effect by the changing glaciers. I want to do some additional research online, talk to the scientists around here some more, then go out on the ice again."

"Fine." His tone suggested it was anything but. He looked from left to right out the windshield, then turned onto the main road. "I'll let Toby know you're interested in another expedition and have him line up someone to take you."

Mariah felt incongruously hurt that he didn't offer to take her himself. "Thanks." She remained silent for most of the ride back to the ranch, except to call to the dogs and thank them, too. And to insist that Patrick stop when she spotted a moose in the woods beside the road that she wanted to photograph.

They soon arrived at their starting point. Wes Dawes was outside with some other dogs, his sledding that day apparently over. Mariah popped out of the van as soon as it stopped, though Patrick came toward her side to help her out.

"Thank you," she said again, looking into those hot light brown eyes with their unfathomable expression. "See you around."

Did a hint of sorrow at her brush-off momentarily cross his face? No, she was just projecting. She turned, arranged her tote bag on her shoulder, and crunched her way over the driveway to say hi to Wes.

That evening, Patrick invited Wes and Shaun to join him in town for a drink. Toby, too. He had already returned from his meeting in Nome. He had flown there and back in a small, private plane—a major way of getting around in Alaska, where towns were spaced so far apart.

They drove in separate vehicles. Shaun had told Patrick that his online research on backgrounds of glaciers, and investigations of them by some scientists who had previously visited Tagoga or who were now in town, seemed to be yielding interesting results. *Very* interesting, in fact, but he refused to elaborate until he had followed some threads to their ends. He wanted to return to his research as soon as possible, since he would have little time with it the next day, when he was scheduled to take some tourists on a sled.

Plus, they had already decided that Patrick would spend the next evening on the glaciers in wolf form. His daytime visits as a musher hadn't yielded much information so far. Shaun would need to be there as his backup.

They wound up at Fiske's Hangout, supposedly the best place in town for a drink and dinner despite the existence of similar nearby bars.

But Patrick wasn't really fooling himself. He hoped that Emil Charteris would be there for him to try to question again. But mostly, he hoped that Mariah would be there talking with Emil. Or even on her own.

When he spotted her, his insides leaped. She wasn't with Emil, though, but hanging out with another scientist Patrick had met before, one only too happy to share the fruit of his investigations—not that Patrick could rely on them. Flynn Shulster seemed more of a pseudo-scientist than a real one. His television show on the Science Channel featured all kinds of unusual nature events.

Patrick wondered if Mariah's articles were ever similar to Shulster's Alaskan tales. He wanted to read one. More likely, they were not like Shulster's at all. From her attitude, he had a sense that Mariah would go out of her way to ensure accuracy in her articles, but Shulster seemed all about sensationalism.

Which was undoubtedly why he was here looking into the untimely retreat of the glaciers.

Since that was why Patrick was here, too, he led his group toward the area of the ornate bar where Shulster held court, Mariah sitting next to him.

"Hi, mushers," Shulster called over the piano music when he spotted them. He had obviously been drinking. He was dressed in a snazzy blue-and-black sweater over snug black slacks. Patrick supposed he was decent-looking, in a show-biz kind of way, with his light brown hair short and styled, his face bright-eyed and smiling. Which was what he was: more appearance than substance. "You didn't bring your dogs."

"I suspect Thea Fiske wouldn't be too happy if I did," Patrick responded.

Shulster returned to the tale he had been spinning to his rapt audience of local drinkers and tourists, all about his experiences in the Himalayas looking for yetis. Nothing about his examination of the local glaciers, though. So nothing interesting to Patrick.

He edged over to Mariah. "Hi," he said in a low voice.

"Hello, Patrick." Her tone sounded welcoming—a surprise, considering the less than amiable way they had parted earlier. "What a surprise to see you here." He heard the drollness in her voice and smiled.

"I could say the same. Have you eaten yet?" He wasn't sure why he asked. Was he going to invite her to join them, like he wanted to turn this chance— well, not so chance—meeting into a date?

"Yes, I have," she said. "I stuck around because I'm interested in hearing what Flynn has to say."

So was Patrick, eventually, after he'd eaten a barbecue sandwich and drunk a couple of beers with Shaun and the Daweses. Shaun headed off to talk to some other bar patrons as Shulster started describing what he had seen so far on the local glaciers.

Which meant Patrick had to hang out longer as the conversation segued into discussions of what others had seen and experienced. He stayed when the Daweses left because Toby was exhausted after his day traveling to Nome and back—and when Shaun excused himself, to resume his online research.

And when Flynn Shulster left, as well as some of the waitstaff and even the piano player. Patrick told himself he was staying to listen to other patrons' tales of glacier experiences. Some stories weren't as interesting as he had hoped. The bar customers, in various states of inebriation, seemed to want to outdo one another in their descriptions—not only of the calving, but of things they had seen regarding the effects on wildlife—and were urged to focus on the facts by Mariah.

But when Mariah decided it was time to leave, though the place was still far from empty, Patrick figured he'd heard enough, too.

Outside in the cold, Mariah turned to him. "Are you walking me back to my B and B tonight?" It sounded like a challenge, not a request, and the look she turned on him with her glowing blue eyes appeared anything but welcoming.

"Sure," he said. "Just want to make certain you arrive safely. With all those guys having a good time in there, you never know when one'll try to follow you home."

"Like you." She smiled briefly and started walking in the direction of her inn. "So, are you going to tell me more about your background tonight—stuff you wouldn't talk about yesterday?"

"No," he said.

"I'm going to keep asking."

"And I'm going to keep avoiding the question."

She laughed. "I figured." Instead of pressing him,

she asked more detailed questions about things they had seen on the glaciers that day, and the care and training of sled dogs.

When they reached her B and B, Patrick hesitated. Lord, how he wanted to grab her and kiss her again. Turn it into a habit.

But that made no sense, given this woman's professional curiosity and his need for secrecy.

"See you around," he said.

Which was when she grabbed his arm, reached up to pull his head down, and planted one hell of a quick but sexy kiss on his lips.

And then she disappeared inside the inn.

Patrick had driven to town in the sedan the military had supplied him with. He took the roads back to the dogsled ranch as fast as possible without killing himself or anyone else.

Why had he decided, in some split second of chivalry and self-preservation, not to kiss Mariah?

And why had she kissed him anyway?

The touch of her lips had driven him nearly wild. Her scent intoxicated him more than all the beer he had drunk in Alaska. He felt as if he had engulfed a small swallow of the elixir that allowed him to turn wolfen on demand, had turned instantly into the wild animal within him.

Had wanted to claim her, take her to a secluded place and make love to her all night.

It was a good thing she had fled inside—wasn't it?

Somehow, fortunately, he made it to the ranch without swerving off the road. He pulled into the parking area behind the main house. The Daweses' car was there, and so was Shaun's crossover. Lights were on in both the house and the large building behind it where the hands' small apartments were located—his destination.

Inside, Patrick ran up the steps to his second-floor unit without seeing any of the other guys. Not surprising. It was late. And most of the time, if he saw them at all here, it was when they gathered downstairs in the small kitchen for coffee or a beer.

He felt too wired to sleep. To even stay in one place.

Good thing Duke would require a short walk before bed.

Patrick used a key to open the door to his apartment. Duke was waiting right inside the door, having obviously heard his arrival.

"Hi, boy," Patrick said, stooping to give his large, gray friend a rough hug. "How ya doing?" He considered Duke much more than a friend. The dog was part of his cover, so that if anyone happened to see Patrick in wolf form he could laugh and say they must have spotted Duke. But Duke was also his companion, apartment mate and buddy. Not to mention a trained canine military partner.

Now, Duke didn't hold still long enough for Patrick to do more than touch his thick fur. He ran into the hall and barked.

"Hush!" Patrick said. He didn't want the dog to wake the other guys this late, or he'd never hear the end of it.

Duke stopped outside Shaun's unit, woofing softly and leaping against the door.

"What's wrong, boy?" Patrick knocked on Shaun's door. Hearing nothing from inside, he turned the knob.

The door opened. Odd. Though guys around here often failed to lock up during the day or night, that didn't include Shaun.

Not with his valuable, government-issue computer equipment.

The sharp, ugly smells assaulted Patrick immediately. "Hey, Shaun," he called warily into the darkness, even as Duke sped by and started making strange, keening noises.

With an eerie, sick sensation crawling up his back, Patrick turned on the light.

Shaun was at the small table at the side of the compact room that passed as multipurpose kitchenette, office and living room. Slumped over. Head on the table.

Blood pooled around him on the floor. Duke sat, howling softly nearby.

"Hell!" Patrick exclaimed. "Shaun?" He crossed the room, touched the neck of his friend and backup, hunting for a pulse.

There was none.

Shaun was dead.

And Patrick realized that the laptop computer that Shaun always worked on at that table was missing.

Chapter 4

Shaun hadn't changed clothes from their outing at Fiske's and still had on his blue cotton shirt. He'd obviously been in a hurry to get back to work, since he usually wore only ratty jeans and T-shirts while on the computer. What had gotten him so jazzed?

Carefully, Patrick repositioned Shaun just a little so he could view his body, assess the wound that killed him.

Only then did Patrick realize how much blood now covered his own hand that had sought a pulse.

Shaun's throat had been cut.

"Damn it, Shaun," Patrick whispered angrily. "How could anyone have done that to you?"

Shaun had been a large, muscular guy. Trained in military hand-to-hand combat. He wouldn't have gotten his throat slit easily.

Except by complete surprise.

Duke would have barked at the intruder. But Duke barked often when mushers entered the building, so Shaun wouldn't have been concerned. Could it have been a fellow musher who killed him?

Almost wishing he was in wolf form so he could howl with Duke—who now sat near the door of the small room issuing low, plaintive keens—Patrick carefully inhaled, and realized he had all but held his breath after that first assault on his senses.

Which might have been a good idea to continue. The odor was horrible, and not just the usual scents involved with the death of a human being.

Something pungently sharp and bleachlike, overlain with the sweetness of some cleaning potion, filled the air. As if the killer had known there would be those with extraordinary senses of smell who might enter the crime scene.

Unsurprising, though, on a ranch where more than thirty dogs lived.

But that could also indicate that the dogs would otherwise have been able to recognize the killer from his—or her—scent.

Patrick needed to report this immediately to Alpha Force. A member of his unit—his pack—had been slain. But he couldn't do anything that appeared suspicious, like making phone calls before notifying the authorities, or he could be accused of Shaun's murder. Knowledge of his affiliation with the military couldn't go any further than it already had, with Wes Dawes aware of it—although Wes knew nothing specific about Alpha Force.

So, first thing, Patrick called 9-1-1, after gingerly removing his cell phone from his pocket with his left hand, not wanting to smear any more blood on himself than he already had.

He explained the situation briefly to the operator, giving his location. Then he called the Daweses. They would need to know that the cops were coming. And why. And what had happened to one of their supposed employees.

Only then did he call his superior officer, Major Drew Connell, of Alpha Force. Woke him up, since he was at Ft. Lukman, in Maryland, a four-hour time difference.

"Don't have time to discuss it now, Drew," he said grimly. "I'll call back as soon as I can. But Shaun's been murdered."

"What the hell—" Drew began. "How? Do you know who?"

"Like I said," Patrick repeated as the Daweses burst into the room, "I'll call you." And then he hung up. "Stay right there," he told the father and son who appeared equally ashen. "We can't contaminate the crime scene any more than I've already done. Don't you watch those shows on TV?" He added the last as an attempt to disavow any connection with law enforcement, however remote, at least as far as Toby was concerned. But he caught Wes's eye and shot him a brief, silent message to keep what he knew quiet.

Another conversation to have later, without an audience.

The cops must have been on patrol in this small town where crime couldn't be too prevalent, since a couple of uniformed officers arrived only five minutes later. They did the usual things like securing the crime scene and sequestering possible witnesses.

By then, the other four guys who lived in the tiny apartments in the building had all been awakened and, in various stages of undress, had gathered in the narrow hall, asking questions of one another. But none apparently had any answers, so as Patrick was being escorted past them by a cop, one of them— Hank Meyer—demanded, "Hey, Worley, what the hell's going on?"

"Shaun's dead," he replied tersely, and didn't need the cop's gentle shove to keep moving. He wasn't about to say anything else. Especially nothing about how he'd found Shaun, or the condition of his body, or all he had sensed. He had a right to remain silent and intended to exercise it—at least until he was cleared of suspicion.

The cop who'd accompanied him outside sat Patrick down in the backseat of his navy-and-white patrol car with the Tagoga Police sign on the side. "A few questions for you, sir." His name tag read Pilke, and he did, fortunately, have only a few questions, at least for now. At his urging, Patrick described where he had been that evening, when he'd last seen Shaun alive, how he had found him. The cop recorded the conversation and took notes.

As Patrick spoke, he watched others from the ranch, including the Daweses, also escorted outside and questioned—beneath the light of a bright and waxing, but fortunately not yet full, moon.

He wondered if any of them knew more than him.

If any was Shaun's murderer.

Whether or not these cops were efficient, Patrick would find the killer. Using any and all resources he had.

He was glad when the cop was finally done with him—after confirming Patrick's employment here and his cell phone number. Patrick wanted to demand that they keep him informed about their crime scene investigation and when they zeroed in on any suspects, but to act that way would raise questions about who the hell he thought he was.

And so he simply thanked the guy, made a dorky comment about how he hoped they caught the killer soon, and exited the vehicle.

He couldn't stay at the ranch that night. The building housing his apartment, and the others', would be at a minimum noisy, and would all most likely be treated as part of the crime scene.

He headed for his car. And wondered whether Inez's B and B had any rooms available.

On his short drive to town, Patrick called Drew Connell again. "What the hell happened there?" the major demanded immediately, as if he had been clutching his cell phone from the moment he'd hung up with Patrick.

Driving slowly along the dark, winding two-lane highway, Patrick described it briefly—how Shaun had been with him at Fiske's, had left early because he wanted to get back to his online research... and sometime between the time he'd left the bar/ restaurant and when Patrick had arrived back there, had had his throat slit.

"Any sign of a struggle?" Drew demanded.

"You know...knew Shaun. The only way someone could have done that was to sneak up on him."

"Yeah."

Patrick described the smell of the cleaning agent and his assumption that it was to prevent the dogs from IDing the killer. "No indication anyone here had any idea about Alpha Force or Shaun's connection with me. But I'll keep looking into what happened to him. And...well, I was planning on heading up to the glaciers again. The last time I was there while it shifted, I heard and saw some stuff I couldn't explain. But without Shaun... Can you send someone else to be my backup?"

"'Fraid you're on your own for now. I've got everyone who could otherwise be your assistant on the road with the other guys here. Something's going on in the lower forty-eight, mine explosions we've been asked to look into, and all our shifters who can navigate small spaces in the dark—nearly half our troops—have been commandeered to work on it. And the other half's their backup."

"Mine explosions?"

"Yeah, as in sources for minerals used to create necessary military ordnance, for one thing. We're not sure what's going on, but some of the heads of the mining companies have asked the military to look into it, and General Yarrow volunteered us."

Patrick shook his head slowly. "So the upshot is that I'm the lone wolf around here."

"We can enlist your bud Wes Dawes to help out to some extent."

As Patrick turned a corner, the lights of town— such as they were at this hour—started to appear. "Not much of an extent now," he cautioned. "Wes could be a suspect in Shaun's murder, although I don't know of any motive. But I can't eliminate anyone yet."

"Got it. He's former military and his security clearance is still adequate for you to enlist what help you think is appropriate, on a limited basis. But— well, you said it. For now, you're the lone wolf."

The room to which the sleepy receptionist directed Patrick was at the rear of the main floor of the B and B.

He wondered if it was near Mariah's.

He didn't ask, though. It would be better if he didn't run into her, if she didn't even know he was around. The curious writer might point her nose in the direction of Shaun's murder—and possibly learn that Patrick had been acquainted with Shaun even before they'd arrived in Tagoga.

He wished he had Duke with him, but had left his surviving partner at the ranch. Duke would be better off there as part of the pack of huskies. And Patrick hadn't been certain where he would end up that night. This way, he hadn't had to grovel to get a dog admitted as a guest at the B and B, and it was one of very few choices in town.

After finishing the details of checking in, he grabbed the thick strap of the backpack he had filled hastily before leaving his apartment and started down the hallway.

And stopped at the first closed door. It had a window inlaid at the top, and the room beyond was the inn's small business center, where two desktop computers were set up. Mariah sat at one of them, watching the screen intensely as her fingers typed nonstop on the keyboard. Her dark hair was loose around her shoulders, mussed as if she'd run her fingers through it…and the thought made Patrick's fingers itch to do the same. Her green sweatshirt hugged her curves.

He should move on before she spotted him. But almost without thinking, Patrick opened the door. He must have startled her, since she gasped and stopped typing, turning toward him.

"Oh, hi, Patrick," she said.

He realized he was grinning foolishly at her and made himself frown. "Don't tell me you're working this late." He glanced down at his watch. Two o'clock. He had left her here nearly three hours ago. Had she been on the computer all that time?

"Okay, I won't tell you." Her lopsided smile was wry. Then her gaze moved from his face to his side, where his backpack hung. Confusion wrinkled the lovely features of her face. "What are you doing here?"

His body grew rigid as his mind focused again on

why he had wound up at Inez's. "Long story," he said curtly. At her instantly irritated expression, he said, "Sorry. Hard to think about it." He told her about Shaun's death. No details—only that someone had killed his friend.

"Oh, Patrick, I'm so sorry." She was immediately on her feet. "And you…you found him?"

"Yeah."

"What happened to him?"

"I don't want to talk about it. What're you working on?" Time to change the subject. Better yet, leave before she pried anything out of him. But he couldn't bring himself just to walk out.

He would either have to weigh every word he spoke, or stay quiet.

For now, he leaned against the door jamb.

"I did more online research about some of the scientists visiting here and their work," she said. "I need to prepare for the next questions I'll ask for my article. There's no internet access available in the rooms, though, so I had to work here. I was just preparing an email progress report for my editor." She hesitated. "Patrick, I don't want to pry, but—"

"Then don't," he said gruffly. Was she about to turn into a nosy investigative reporter, demand more answers about Shaun that he wasn't prepared to give? Worse, answers he didn't have yet and was chewing himself out about, for not having been there for his friend. He was even more frustrated that he couldn't leap into conducting his own investigation, his way, with the cops all over the place.

She glanced at the computer screen and pressed a button on the mouse, probably sending her email. She rose and turned back toward him. "What I was going to say—as tactfully as I can, but that's now out of the question—is that you look awful. Tired. And really upset. If it weren't so late, I'd invite you to join me for a drink. But nothing's open around here, and—"

"Rain check," he said. "You're right. I'm tired. You must be, as well. I'm heading for my bed, and you should, too." He realized she could take that wrong... or maybe not so wrong. "To your bed, I mean."

There was that wry smile again. And something else that smoldered in her sea-blue eyes. "Right," she said. "Good night, Patrick. I'm planning to check out some of the resources in town tomorrow morning, so I'll be at breakfast around eight-thirty. Maybe I'll see you then."

She sat back down at the computer. He watched for a moment, changing his position so the angle allowed him to see that she was logging off. And he didn't necessarily want to continue this conversation with her...now.

"Good night, Mariah," he said, and headed down the hall toward his room.

* * *

Thank heavens he was gone, Mariah thought a moment later as she shut down the computer.

Otherwise, she might have said something equally dumb herself. Like taking him up on his obviously unintentional offer to join him in his bed.

But not tonight. His friend had died. Shaun Bethune. He'd seemed nice enough when she'd talked with him at Fiske's, not that they'd said more than a few friendly words to one another.

And now, he was dead. Apparently murdered.

By whom? And why? A robbery gone bad? But he'd been another employee at the dogsled ranch. Unlikely that he had a lot worth stealing.

Patrick clearly needed some cheering up. But not by her. At least not tonight.

Tomorrow? She'd have to see.

The guy was hot. No doubt about that. And she'd enjoyed his company the few times they had been together, despite his initial unwelcoming attitude at the dogsled ranch, and his obvious reluctance to take her on another trek onto the glaciers.

He had kissed her, sure. Accepted her kiss. But he hadn't pursued anything—probably for the best. He wasn't really interested in her, and she shouldn't be interested in him. She sighed as she walked out of the office center and closed the door behind her.

Her room was on the next floor, so she headed

toward the reception area where the stairs were located.

And felt a little creeped out. The lights here were low. No one waited behind the inn's small reception desk for people to check-in, not at this hour.

The place was quiet, too. The only sound she heard was warm air blowing through the heating system.

She felt like running to her room, but just stepped up her pace toward the stairway past the desk. Whoever killed Shaun wasn't likely to be at Inez's. But from what she'd gathered from Patrick, the authorities hadn't yet zeroed in on a suspect, so how could she know for sure?

"You okay?" said a voice from behind, startling her. She must have jumped a foot.

She pivoted. Patrick stood there.

"What are you doing here?" she demanded, her body shaking.

"I dropped my stuff in my room but figured... well, I thought you might want someone to walk you to yours. Didn't mean to scare you." He looked chastened, like a young boy who'd been chewed out for pulling a girl's hair.

"It's okay," she said as her trembling stopped. "And you're right. I'd appreciate some company. Everyone around here'll be nervous as word gets out about what happened to Shaun."

"Yeah." His expression shuttered again. Poor

guy. Obviously in pain, yet not willing to show his emotions.

"I'm upstairs," she said gently. "This way." And realized that, like he had done before, she'd said something that could be misinterpreted as an invitation for more than a stroll to her door.

That would have made her smile under other circumstances. But games like that were not appropriate tonight.

She headed up the stairway, glad to hear his footsteps behind her.

The hallway upstairs was dimly lit. Her room was nearly at the end. When she got there, she reached into her pocket, extracted her key and unlocked the door.

She turned back toward Patrick. "Thanks for walking me here," she whispered, not wanting to disturb other guests. "And...well, if there's anything I can do to help about Shaun, please let me know."

His expression was bleak. She wanted in the worst way to cheer him.

Almost involuntarily, she stood up on her toes and kissed him. Gently. On the mouth. Not quite sisterly, but not suggestive, either.

He responded immediately. His arms went around her, and she was suddenly in the middle of a torrid embrace that made her gasp. His kiss grew so sexy that it nearly made her knees buckle. She considered tugging him into her room.

But he pulled away abruptly. A light in his amber eyes suggested that he, too, was more than a little aroused.

Even so… "Good night again," he said and strode off down the hall.

Patrick slept only about an hour that night.

His bed at the B and B was comfortable enough. His state of mind was not.

Lying awake in almost complete darkness, beneath the duvet in the room that smelled of pine-scented cleaning solutions, he thought a lot—too much— about Mariah. She was in the same building, one floor away.

He imagined what she looked like in bed. He remembered that not-so-chaste kiss. And their couple of prior kisses—too short, yet arousing.

He had to get away, stay far away, from the woman who wrote about animals. Not just sleep in a different building from her.

He also thought about Shaun. His murder. The blood.

The sights, the sounds, the smells around the sled hands' house.

How he'd failed to pick up clues as to the identity

of the murderer. And how the killer had obscured potentially useful evidence, like a scent.

If Patrick hadn't been sure the cops would still be around, he'd have sneaked back under the cover of darkness early this morning. He'd still head there a little later, after checking out of the B and B. Maybe that wasn't the best decision. Normal people would stay in a nice, comfy inn, out of the way of a murder investigation.

He wasn't normal people.

He had to look like one, though, so his excuse would be that he needed to be at the ranch for the dogs' sake, which was true.

But when he was alone, near enough to accomplish his real goal, he would extract the most important contents of his backpack: the elixir and the light that triggered its usefulness.

As a wolf, he would be able to use enhanced senses to find any trace the murderer had left—and there was bound to be something, at least tonight, when the kill was so fresh.

Because he could not be there alone tonight, the best Patrick could hope for was that the crime scene guys found everything there was to find and handled it perfectly.

Unlikely.

So it would be better from his perspective if they found nothing at all.

At least they might not still be hanging out there collecting evidence tomorrow night. If so, that would give Patrick his opportunity to conduct his own hunt for clues pointing to Shaun's murderer.

While he shifted into his wolf form.

Chapter 5

The moment she opened her eyes that morning, Mariah was wide awake. She immediately headed for the shower in the small bathroom attached to her room.

Her first thoughts were of Patrick Worley, and seeing him in the business center the night before. He had been sweet, walking her to her room, despite his own grieving, when she'd felt so freaked out about the murder of his friend.

Poor Shaun. She'd barely met him, but he seemed nice enough. Why would anyone have killed him— and as brutally as Patrick had hesitated to describe? And in this small town, where residents probably knew everyone else who lived here. Her curiosity was on high alert. Shaun had worked at the same dogsled ranch as Patrick. Did that have anything to do with why he died?

Unlikely, but she would consider writing a separate article on the ranch, its dogs and its mushers—and use it as an excuse to look into Shaun's murder, as long as her new research didn't interfere with her nature article. Her boss, who owned more than one publication, would love that.

But poor Patrick, too. Shaun's death had clearly been hard on him. She would have to see if there was anything she could do to help him through this difficult situation…within reason.

For her own sake, though, she should probably stay away from him.

She'd dreamed about him. She couldn't quite remember her nighttime fantasy, but judging by the sensitivity of her body this morning, it had been steamy. Or maybe that was actually a daylight reaction, resulting from her ongoing attraction to him.

Which was absurd. Yes, he was one hot guy. Maybe she should satisfy her curiosity, indulge in a one-night stand. That might even help him get his mind off his friend's death, too, for a little while. Do a good deed both for herself and for him.

But what if, instead of feeling satisfied, she only wanted more?

After showering, she fixed her hair, put on a minimal amount of makeup, and dressed nicely but casually. She had a meeting later with the science teacher at the town's high school, for a local perspective on wildlife.

When she was ready to go, she glanced at the clock on the bedside table. Eight-thirty, the time she'd told Patrick she'd be at breakfast.

After locking her door, she hurried downstairs.

The inn's breakfast area was crowded but not full. The room sounded alive with low conversation and the clinking of plates. About a dozen people were seated at small wooden tables, alone and in groups of two and three.

Patrick wasn't there.

Mariah went to get her food—wheat toast with strawberry jam, a hard-boiled egg, orange juice and coffee. Then she had to decide where to sit. With others…or alone at a table for two?

Before she'd decided, she saw Patrick fill the doorway, his backpack again over his shoulder. He wore his heavy jacket, unzipped to reveal a gold sweater beneath.

He joined her near the toaster. "Morning," he said. "I thought I'd find you here. I'm checking out now and not staying for breakfast."

"Oh?" She put her food down on the counter, feeling ridiculously hurt, as if he'd stood her up for a date.

"I want to get back to the dogs, Duke and all of them. I'm sure they're upset. Though they're unlikely to understand that Shaun's dead, there was a lot of activity around them last night. And Toby and Wes were probably kept too busy to pay much attention to them."

"I understand." And she did. She might have the sense that Patrick chose not to relate to people at times, but she could definitely identify with people who cared for animals.

Her mind immediately returned to that wolf on the glacier, and she thrust the thought away. Why go there now?

"If I can do anything to help them, or the Daweses," she said, "please let me know. And I still hope you'll take me back out on the glaciers—maybe tomorrow, if the ranch is up and running again." *Then* she could worry about that wolf.

His eyes bored into hers. "I told you I'd let Toby know you wanted someone to take you out again."

She was not intimidated. "And I told you I'd like it to be you." She crossed her arms, waiting for the next salvo.

It came as a broad, sexy grin that nearly made her knees buckle. "We'll see," he said, then left the room.

* * *

Driving through wind-whipped snow flurries, Patrick called Wes on his way back to the dogsled ranch. "Cops gone?" he asked. "Are we working today?"

"Yes and yes," was the reply. "We're still under orders to cooperate with the investigators and keep everyone out of Shaun's room, but otherwise we're supposedly back to normal. Except for the fact that we're missing a musher—and we're all still suspects."

"Got it. The dogs handling it okay?"

"I guess. You can figure it out…when you're back."

There was a hint of inquiry in the last, so Patrick responded, "On my way."

"Oh, and Patrick?"

"Yeah?"

"I know Shaun was your friend," Wes said. "I didn't know him well, but he seemed like a good guy. We'll miss him around here."

"Yeah."

Patrick arrived at the ranch ten minutes later, parked in the area designated for staff and headed to the large building where the dogs were housed when not out romping or working.

Duke came over to him, whined and waited for Patrick to kneel and stroke him. Duke and he had been partners for a while now. The dog had been acquired by Alpha Force as a pup and designated as Patrick's cover over a year ago—because he was a combination shepherd-wolfhound that looked a lot like Patrick's shifted form.

"Good boy," Patrick said, then, more softly into the dog's ear, "Looks like we're on our own."

But when his cell phone rang only a minute later, that situation changed.

"Can you talk now?" Major Drew Connell asked.

Standing, Patrick said, "Just me and the dogs at the moment."

"Good. Here's the deal. I've already spoken with Wes Dawes, since you and I discussed it."

When Drew was done talking, Patrick gave Duke a pat and headed out the door toward the main house. As he walked inside the entry, he heard someone speaking in the kitchen. It was Wes, who hung up his cell phone as Patrick walked into the room.

"Sounds like you and me have some talking to do," Wes said, grinning.

"Got some time now?"

They sat at the kitchen table, Patrick with a glass of orange juice and Wes with coffee.

Wes looked like a junior version of his dad, muscular, not too tall, with a round face and receding hairline. His gray sweater was threadbare around the elbows and sleeves. His expression was sober. "Give me a heads-up on what you'll expect from me."

"We can't officially recruit you into Alpha Force," Patrick said. "Because you're not in the military any longer. But since you had a high clearance, I can rely on you for backup. Did Major Connell explain our mission?"

Even if he had, Patrick was certain that Drew would not have revealed the true nature of Alpha Force. Not only was Wes nonmilitary, he had also not been ruled out as a suspect in Shaun's murder.

But Patrick might need backup as he investigated the disappearing glaciers, and that was what, in generalities, he revealed to Wes.

"That was one reason for our partying so much at Fiske's," Patrick confirmed to Wes. "To talk to the scientists hanging out there in a relaxed setting, where they won't know how interested we are in their answers."

"Got it. What else?"

"We'll wing it. Glad you're on board."

Wes might be a real asset, since he knew people around here. Some of what Patrick needed to accomplish involved learning people's observations about the glaciers.

Tonight, though, when Patrick visited Great Glaciers National Park in wolf form, he would be on his own.

* * *

Mariah had time to kill before meeting with the local science teacher. She knew exactly where she wanted to go: the closest place that had Wi-Fi. The internet connection in the business center at her little B and B had worked out okay last night, but it was slow.

Besides, she wanted to use her own laptop for ease of storing information she found during her research.

Most of all, she wanted to be sure no one could see, in some menu of last topics researched, exactly what she was looking for.

She would walk to the Tagoga Library. It wasn't far from Inez's B and B. And if she made a call on the way, her conversation wouldn't be overheard.

She bundled up and started outside. Walking wasn't the safest thing to do on slick sidewalks during heavy snow flurries, but she used her cell to phone her boss, the editor of *Alaskan Nature Magazine,* among other publications. "Hi, Harold." She snugged the receiver against her ear beneath her knit cap.

Harold Hanrahan wasn't much older than Mariah's age of thirty-one. He had taken over his family's publishing company when his father, its founder, had had enough of Alaska's winters and moved to Florida. Harold had already been an editor, and he was also an excellent businessman. In addition to

Alaskan Nature, he now owned a weekly publication distributed in several small towns—filled with lots of advertising—and a monthly rag that focused on gossip and celebrity sensationalism.

Neither was to Mariah's taste, but she occasionally wrote articles for them, on Harold's request. After all, she'd written similar swill in her past. And under Harold's tenure, subscriptions to *Alaskan Nature* had tripled. Its distribution outlets all over the country now included not only standard places like newsstands but also unusual ones like pet stores, animal rescue organizations and even stores that sold sporting goods and outdoor gear.

"So tell me more about that murder," he said with no preamble.

"I doubt it has anything to do with the article I'm researching," she retorted wryly, but she nevertheless told him all she knew—which wasn't much. "But that's one reason I'm calling," she said. "I intend to look a little more closely into what's going on around here. If I see anything we can use for a cover story relating not only to wildlife, but anything touching on natural occurrences around here, I'll follow up."

"*Un*natural occurrences, too," he said gruffly. "Write about anything juicy you find out about the killing, and I'll include your article in the *Advertiser* or the *Journal,* whichever works best."

It was the response she had anticipated, she

reflected as she hung up and carefully stuck her phone into her purse with one hand. Her other hand held her laptop's case, and both were covered in bulky, warm gloves.

And though she really didn't want to get into the details of Shaun's death, she could now justify spending time researching it to see where it led.

More info about Patrick Worley? Maybe. They'd clearly been friends.

She reached the Tagoga Library. Fortunately, despite the smallness of the town and compactness of its library, it was advanced enough to make Wi-Fi available to its patrons.

Nearly filled bookshelves lined the room, sur-rounding about a dozen small tables. The place wasn't crowded, and after waving a greeting to the librarian on duty, she chose a table as far from the door as possible to set up her computer.

After removing her gloves and jacket, and rubbing her hands together to warm them in the comfortable heat of the library, Mariah sat down and started to work.

First, she did a Google search on Shaun Bethune, to see if she could learn anything more about him than she'd found on the inn's computer last night—like what he'd done before working at the Great Glaciers Dogsled Ranch. She'd gotten the impression he hadn't been there much longer than Patrick, an apparent newcomer.

She found nothing on anyone she thought could be this Shaun. Few people with his name were listed, and the ages, and circumstances of their listings didn't sound like the man who had just died.

An apparent dead end—and she didn't intend the pun. But that didn't mean she couldn't learn anything about him. Her research would have to be done here in Tagoga, subtly. And without interfering with her researching the article she really wanted to write.

She had one more person to research before looking for information about local schools, to prepare for her interview later.

She looked up Patrick Worley. She had an excuse to check Shaun on Google: a writer's investigative curiosity. But her reason to look up Patrick on the internet was simply that she was interested.

She found quite a few people with his name, including businessmen and scientists, medical doctors and educators—but none that sounded like him.

Until she came to a Patrick Worley who was the survivor of two deceased Maryland citizens, including a veterinarian. If this was him, he had come by his love of dogs naturally.

Only…how odd! The stuff she found on various websites—including pages devoted to the town of Mary Glen, where the vet's practice had been—was full of allusions to local legends. Werewolves, of all things!

Of course that had been discredited. There had been some odd goings-on in the town, including the murder of that Patrick Worley's dad and mother, too. But the killer had been found.

Nothing for Mariah to use, most certainly not in her article on local wildlife in the Tagoga, Alaska, area. Or even a story on the death of Shaun Bethune.

But this could certainly explain why Patrick was so closemouthed about his background. Who would want to admit to having had his world shaken up by a bunch of woo-woo, credulous fruitcakes?

And Patrick—there were a couple of mentions of the surviving son, and the fact he had enlisted in the military but was dishonorably discharged.

Her Patrick?

There was no explanation of the circumstances. And she couldn't even be certain that it was the right Patrick Worley.

Even if it was, that didn't matter.

Mariah had an article on local wildlife to research and write. And she would keep that focus at the forefront of her mind.

Patrick was again—still—on Mariah's mind a few hours later after her appointment with John Amory, the Tagoga High School science teacher who taught biology and advanced biology classes.

She needed Patrick, or at least his dogsled team. She was completely jazzed about getting back onto the glaciers as quickly as possible.

That was why she'd decided to go to Fiske's this evening for dinner, in the hope of running into Patrick there. But after the death of his friend, was he likely to be eating out in such a noisy, jovial place?

She didn't know, but, snugging her jacket around her, she set out walking briskly from Inez's, in the dark after sunset, toward the restaurant/bar.

In her mind, she rehashed her interview with the science teacher. John Amory had been a gold mine of information, and Mariah had taken copious notes on his ruminations about all kinds of Alaskan wildlife he had seen on the glaciers and elsewhere around here during the past ten years. His favorite part of each school year, he'd told her, was to take students on field trips onto the glaciers, see what kind of animals were there during which season, and take pictures.

He had even made copies of a lot of pictures for her and gave her a release so she could publish them.

And now, she was all but drooling to go back to Great Glaciers National Park and take more photos of her own. Use identifiable landmarks in John's pictures and shoot some in the same locations.

Maybe she could even capture some of the same kinds of animals. But she suspected, because of the frightening changes to the area of the glaciers, she was more likely to find at least some of those areas barren of life.

Maybe, though, she would see that wolf again.

She laughed a little at herself. Why was she getting so obsessed about that animal?

Pushing open the door to Fiske's, she heard the roar of conversations inside. When she gazed around, she didn't see Patrick or anyone else from the dogsled ranch.

Darn. Well, she wasn't really surprised. And when she backed outside again to call, just in case, she only got the Great Glaciers Dogsled Ranch answering machine, the recorded voice telling her to leave a message.

Instead, she decided to head to the ranch and talk to someone—hopefully Patrick, but one of the Daweses would do—once she finished dinner.

And then, shivering from the cold, she went back inside.

Emil Charteris and his family were seated at a table. She headed there, glad to see at least a few familiar faces in the loud crowd. They made room for her, and she put her jacket over the back of her chair and sat down. When Thea came over, Mariah ordered what was becoming her usual here—warm, spiked cider and salmon.

She was glad to find herself seated between Emil and his son-in-law. Turning to Jeremy, she asked, loudly enough to be heard over the crowd, "How's your wildlife research progressing? Anything you can share with me yet for my article?"

The lines in his forehead deepened as he shook his head and peered at her over his glasses. "We don't have our protocol complete, but my preliminary research seems to indicate things are still stable."

"Really? I got a different opinion a little while ago from the local science teacher." She described her meeting with John Amory and showed some of his photos. "He's planning a field trip with his students soon, but he's been up on the glaciers himself and thinks there aren't nearly the same numbers of animals there that he's used to seeing. I want to visit the areas he photographed as soon as possible to get my own take on them. And what about the statistics you're compiling?" she asked Carrie.

"Nothing helpful yet, but I'm working on it."

"How do you intend to visit the areas in the photos?" Emil asked Mariah.

"Dogsled. It was a wonderful way to get right onto the glaciers when I went there before. Only…well, I'm hoping the Great Glaciers Dogsled Ranch will be available for rides soon. Did you hear what happened there?"

"Is that where the guy was killed?" Carrie's pretty face squeezed into a grimace. "Sounded awful."

"That's the place," Mariah confirmed. "I hope they figure out soon who did it."

"You're a journalist, aren't you?" Jeremy asked. "Are you going to write about the killing?"

"If my editor has his way," she said with a wry shake of her head. "And since he's my boss, he usually does."

"I heard the guy was killed in his room at the dogsled ranch," Carrie said. "Did someone working there do it?"

"Could be," Mariah replied. But no one she'd met there seemed a likely killer…right? Not Patrick, at least. But what did she really know about him?

She was even far from certain that he was the same Patrick Worley she'd found online.

She was glad that the topic of conversation shifted to the weather here and in the lower forty-eight. And when she finished her dinner, she paid her bill and hurried from the restaurant toward the inn, where her car was parked.

Time to go find Patrick.

This wouldn't be easy, Patrick thought.

He wasn't going out on the glaciers tonight after

all. He needed to use every ability he had to find any available clues about who had killed Shaun as soon as possible, before anything that was still there disappeared. And before anyone was permitted by the police to return there to where they lived.

Clues the cops wouldn't find, or would overlook.

Fortunately, the dogsled ranch was isolated, surrounded by mountainous woodlands. The trees would provide only a minimal amount of cover, barren of leaves this late in fall, but the ground was uneven and there were enough places where he could hide and accomplish what he needed to.

He got into his car and drove down the road to avoid leaving human footprints that the cops might see. He'd already scouted an area to park, unnoticed.

He sat in his vehicle for a few minutes nevertheless, checking around in the darkness for any sign of someone following him.

Nothing.

It was time.

He pulled his backpack from the floor of the passenger's side. He extracted the two critical contents: a cloth bag containing the battery-operated light that created artificial illumination resembling moonlight…and the bottle of the special Alpha Force tonic.

He measured some liquid into a plastic cup, also

taken from the bag, and drank it. Amazingly pleasant and ordinary tasting, considering what it was. A hint of lemon, a little mint…and a whole lot more.

He got out of the car. Turned on the light. Stood in its intense glow, watching, waiting…and shut it off while he still could as he started to change.

He felt the strain on his muscles, his internal organs, his skin. Sensed himself shrinking swiftly to ground level, his arms and legs morphing into canine limbs. No pain, lots of sensation, tugging, retraction, growth. Still awareness, thanks to the elixir. Watched through eyes that grew brighter as silvery fur erupted from his skin.

And as the shift grew complete, he used the keenness of his modified hearing to listen to his own triumphant howl.

Fortunately, despite the cold, there was no precipitation, so Mariah's drive to the dogsled ranch was uneventful. When she arrived, she called again from her cell phone, but still got no answer.

The front gate to the driveway was locked, and the main house looked dark. She parked with the nose of her vehicle on the drive and got out to look around. When she pushed the intercom button on the stone pilaster, no one responded.

She heard dogs barking from the house, saw the

building to its rear and the large outbuilding where the teams lived.

And then…what was that appearing from behind the house? Was one of the dogs loose on the property, alone?

The animal stopped, as if it had seen her, too. It looked like a wolf. Resembled the wolf Mariah had seen on the calving glacier two nights earlier. Hey, that was great!

But what an imagination she had. Who said it was the same wolf? Talk about obsession.

And yet…she was somehow convinced it was the same one. And she didn't want to look away. The dog—wolf?—also continued to stare in her direction.

Fortunately, Mariah had slipped her tote bag over her shoulder. Without looking away, she reached inside and groped for her camera. She pulled it out, turned it on. Snapped a picture.

The flash must have startled the animal. It ran away, back behind the house.

When Mariah looked at its picture on her camera's digital screen, she drew in her breath. It definitely looked like a wolf—*the* wolf—at least from this distance.

And she couldn't shake off the idea that its eyes, its thick gray coat, its alert ears…it really had to be the wolf she had seen before.

* * *

She did not belong here. Not now.

His being at the ranch at this moment, in this form, was risky enough. But having the woman who pried for a living here, too…unacceptable.

Yet there was nothing he could do. He had no other person as backup. He had done all to ensure his change would be a short one.

And then he had come here, his senses enhanced, to seek anything to point to who had harmed his friend, Shaun.

Fortunately, no human stayed on the property this night.

But all scents had, in fact, already been masked by the clever killer.

Even outside, on the grounds, he found nothing useful. No smells, footprints, tire tracks, beyond what was expected.

Except the spicy scent of Mariah.

And now, when he wanted to go to the front of the building where Shaun was murdered to continue his quest for anything useful, he couldn't.

Not with Mariah watching him. Taking his picture.

He fled to the backyard.

He should hate the woman for her interference. But, somehow, he didn't.

And that was more disquieting than her staring at him and taking his picture.

With a low howl that he was certain she could hear, loud enough to set the dogs inside barking, he turned and loped from the property.

Chapter 6

Mariah was awake long before the sun came up the next morning, and it wasn't just because the late fall days in Alaska were growing shorter.

She got out of bed. Showered. Started getting dressed. Fast. Preoccupied.

She hadn't slept well. Not with thoughts of poor Shaun Bethune still invading her mind. And, of course, sexy, enigmatic Patrick Worley.

Not to mention that wolf at the dogsled ranch.

A wolf. She loved wildlife. And she was curious. Was it the same wolf?

Why would a wolf get so near a pack of domesticated canines? Was it due to changes to its natural habitat, like the decimation of the glaciers?

Or was it something else? Dissension within his pack? Search for a new one? A lack of prey? Patrick's presence?

If he was the right Patrick Worley and grew up in an area where werewolf legends abounded...

She laughed aloud as she grabbed her tote bag and purse and slammed her room's door closed behind her. What a gullible idiot she was. Werewolves, indeed. Although if there were any such thing, she'd love to meet one. What an article she could do for *Alaskan Nature!* Or, better yet, her boss Harold's gossipy rag.

Now, though, it was time for breakfast. And a good dose of caffeine. And reality.

As always, the inn's breakfast area was crowded but not full. Mariah sat alone at a table for two and eavesdropped.

The cold weather was a big topic of conversation. So was a local sightseeing tour by small airplane. She'd have to look into that.

Some guys at a nearby table talked about the murder of a local musher in low undertones— Shaun. Mariah had the sense they were either in law enforcement, sent here to help the local cops, or they were from the media and knew the right lingo.

In either case, she'd remember their faces and

maybe say hi to them someday, if she thought they could share useful information with her.

She ate fast, filled a paper cup with hot coffee and put a cardboard sleeve around it, then slid on her jacket and went outside.

The temperature was even colder than yesterday. The wind was blowing. She shivered as she hustled to the parking area and got into her SUV.

And headed toward the Great Glaciers Dogsled Ranch. Again.

On the way, she once more tried calling ahead, but still no one answered. She didn't leave a message.

The gate was open, so she pulled into the driveway as she had done a couple of days ago. Like late yesterday, there was no indication of any law enforcement types here.

The place looked peaceful. Not even any dogs in the yard.

Or wolves.

She peered into the woods surrounding the place. The trees were bare and bleak—and appeared empty. She parked, got out and started up the driveway. Oh, yes, the dogs were present. She heard them barking from inside the buildings, both the house and the large enclosed kennel beyond the yard where she had first photographed the huskies.

She'd run into Patrick right there the first time she had visited. No sign of him now, though.

She went to the house's front door and rang the bell. And waited, listening for anything besides the barking of the dogs inside. No sound of any human occupation.

Hearing an engine behind her, she turned to see a vehicle edging around hers and up the driveway.

Patrick wasn't alone in his car. Both of the Daweses were inside, as well. Mariah followed the vehicle's movement along the driveway to the rear of the house.

"What brings you here so early, Mariah?" Toby asked as he exited the vehicle, zipping up his jacket. Wes and Patrick also got out.

"Looking for another dogsled ride, of course," she said cheerfully.

"Yeah, I got your messages, but we were closed for a couple of days." The expression on his unshaven face looked grim beneath his knit cap. "You heard about Shaun, I assume." He stood in front of her, his large shoulders hunched beneath his gray parka.

She nodded. "Patrick told me. I'm so sorry."

"Us, too. Anyway, I might be able to squeeze you in, but since we had to cancel on some of our tour groups I have to reschedule them first."

"Couldn't Patrick take me out right now?" She tried to look the picture of innocence as she smiled toward him.

"That should work," Toby agreed.

"Thought you wanted me to start packing Shaun's things, now that the cops are through?" Patrick's tone suggested that sorting a dead man's possessions would be a whole lot preferable to her company, which caused Mariah's smile to vanish.

"They'll wait," Toby said. "Or Wes can do it."

The expression that crossed Patrick's face suggested momentary alarm, but it disappeared almost immediately. "No, he needs to help you reschedule the tours," he said smoothly, glancing toward a nodding Wes. "Here's the compromise. I'll take Mariah out for a short jaunt now. If she wants more later, we can decide on another day and time. Okay?"

Though Toby was the boss, Patrick's tone didn't leave room for anything but approval. "Sounds good," he said. "Long as it's okay with Mariah."

"It'll do," she said, as an SUV parked beside them and started disgorging guys who were probably the ranch's other mushers.

She looked at them. Could one of these guys have killed Shaun? Surely the cops would have considered that. And it really wasn't her concern, despite her editor, Harold, encouraging her to do a little investigative journalism here.

She eavesdropped on the greetings between the Daweses and their employees. They apparently hadn't seen each other since the police started their investigation. One was named Hank, another Jimmy. None looked like an obvious killer.

But if she happened to learn something useful that was related more to murder than wildlife...

She'd been known to write some pretty incisive factual articles in her past life, before coming to Alaska to enjoy her career more.

Maybe she could do it again.

"So why are we doing this today?" Patrick asked his passenger in the ranch's van. The team of dogs was in the rear compartment with the sled. They were on their way back to the glaciers.

"Because I want to compress more research into less time," Mariah said. "I have to complete my article. My editor is giving me other ideas, although nothing I'm extremely excited about."

Patrick looked toward her. Despite her words, there was an air of excitement in her smile as she watched the ice-covered landscape go by. She had removed the cap she'd worn at the ranch, and her dark hair was mussed becomingly around her face. How could she look so sexy with all those warm clothes on?

"So what's your next topic?" he asked, his eyes back on the slick road.

"If my editor has his way, it'll be something on Shaun's death," she said bluntly.

"For your nature magazine?"

"He owns other publications, too."

More reasons for her to be nosy. Ask questions.

Get in his way—and maybe make it even harder for him to deal with the killer himself—once he figured out who it was.

How was he going to, instead, get her out of his way?

Especially when her presence was such a damned turn-on?

He'd finally reached the area he'd been looking for. He pulled the van onto the side of the road and maneuvered it so he could easily take the dogs and sled from the back.

Before he got out, he said, "So our goal today is the same as last time—looking for wildlife so you can take pictures."

"That, and I want to try to find the landmarks from the photos I got from the high school science teacher, John Amory." She pulled pictures from an envelope extracted from her tote bag. "I want to shoot some of the same areas again if I can find them, compare any animals I find with the ones in these shots. These photos are about a year old, John told me. There are a few rock formations that I'd especially like to find." She pointed to ice-covered crags and castle-turret-like shapes with sheep and bears and various types of birds gathered nearby.

At least one formation appeared familiar, so Patrick knew the first direction to aim the sled.

"Sounds good."

"One more thing. That wolf I saw here the first night. I'm not sure if it's the same one I saw last evening near your ranch, but it could have been. There was certainly a resemblance. That's my number one priority. If we could somehow find him on the glaciers and get his picture, that's what I want to do."

She looked directly at Patrick as if she could read his thoughts. Which were turbulent just then.

"What wolf? And when were you here yesterday?" She didn't know he'd watched her from the ranch last night, while shifted.

"I came by, but no one seemed to be around, so I left." Her stare didn't waver.

She surely didn't believe that the two wolves were the same…and that both were him while shifted? Did she?

Of course not. He shrugged off his uneasiness… almost. "Well, let's go see what we can find." He exited the van.

Outside the vehicle, Mariah enjoyed helping attach the eager huskies to the sled. She gave each of the nine dog team members a hug, especially the lead dog, Mac. And then she dutifully got on in front of

Patrick and assumed the sitting position he'd shown her before.

"Let's go!" he shouted, and they were off.

It was heady. And exhilarating! The cold air slapped at her face, mostly hidden by a scarf that wrapped her nose and mouth beneath her knit cap. The sky was clear, a startling shade of azure, and sunlight sparkled around them without warming the air.

If the huskies were cold under their thick fur coats, or if their feet froze on the snow-dusted ice's surface, they didn't show any discomfort. Instead, they appeared as happy as if they'd been untethered in heaven.

Mariah couldn't see Patrick behind her but was very aware of his presence. And his warmth, as he leaned forward against her back to control the dogs.

Mariah had tried hard to read his expression when she'd mentioned locating a wolf up here. Mostly, he looked irritated. And resigned. No indication he knew anything unusual about either or both animals.

Not that she had actually anticipated something from him. Why should he even understand what she'd been driving at so obliquely, when it had been entirely a figment of her overactive imagination? He'd probably laugh his head off if she hinted more directly that she'd read about werewolves, of all things.

"That picture with the top-hat rock formation," he shouted from behind her. "With the grizzly bear? We'll go there first."

She turned her head and nodded eagerly. "Great," she called, unsure if he could hear her above the rushing wind that was enhanced by their speed.

The surface of the glacier—she believed it was named Akjaq—was relatively flat where they were, but huge icy cliffs rose to their right. The glacier's edge, with the sea below, was half a mile to their left. Mariah drank in the awesome sights. No animals here, though. Would they see any at all on this outing?

In five minutes, without slowing their speed, they reached the area in the photo. Mariah recognized it easily, with the nearly conical rocky outcropping covered with patches of ice sparkling frigidly in the sunlight.

No grizzly bears wandered at its base today, though. Even so, Mariah took some photos after Patrick stopped the sled, and was gratified to spot a bald eagle flying by.

"This is amazing!" she exclaimed to Patrick. Her excitement grew even headier, somehow, when she saw he watched her with a grin that enhanced his gorgeous features. She'd thought him handsome even with his usual expressionless look, but when he smiled...awesome!

She'd taken off her mittens to snap pictures on her digital camera, and her hands were freezing. Even so, she reached into her tote bag for John Amory's photos. "How about this one?" She held up one for Patrick to see. The rock formation in it resembled ice-covered organ pipes.

"Looks like the one near Afalati Glacier," he said.

It took time to get there, skimming over two other wide ice formations on their way. But soon, Mariah again recognized, in the distance, the pattern of tall, rocky crags coated in the ubiquitous Alaskan ice.

To skirt some difficult ice outcroppings, they traveled near the cliff edge of Afalati, overlooking Tagoga Bay far below.

"Let's stop for a minute so I can get some pictures," Mariah called to Patrick.

He apparently couldn't hear. His arm was outstretched as he held the dogsled's reins, so she touched him. "Please stop."

This time, he ordered the dogs, "Whoa." Once they were stopped, he asked her, "You okay?"

She repeated her desire to get pictures before they continued, then got off the sled, camera in hand.

She looked first in the direction they'd been traveling. "Hey, is that a bear?" She pointed toward the base of the craggy outcropping, where a round mound of dark fur moved slowly inland.

"Looks like," Patrick agreed.

"Then I'll get this kind of picture later. Let's go on—as long as the dogs aren't too afraid."

Several members of the team were sitting, but the rest appeared poised to continue.

"They're fine. We'll—"

She didn't hear him finish. Instead, the air around them seemed to explode, then fill with shrill, frantic calls of orcas in distress. But the surface where they stood was probably fifty feet from the water below. Holding her camera ready, Mariah hurried toward the edge, preparing the telephoto setting so she could get the best picture possible.

When she looked down, the water's surface was indeed churning, as if the killer whales were just below, thrashing. That was when Mariah heard loud, explosive noises, followed by cracking sounds so loud that she reached up to hold her ears.

"Run!" Patrick shouted, grabbing her and practically carrying her toward the sled. The dogs were all standing now, and the lead dog, Mac, began to howl. Several others joined him.

"No!" Patrick shoved Mariah onto the sled as he grabbed the driver's handle and hollered to the dogs, "Hike! Let's go!"

They immediately started running, pulling the

sled. Mariah was impressed with their obedience and unanimity, even as she was unnerved by the continuously increasing sounds of fracturing ice.

And then she screamed as she saw a jagged tear form in the glacier's surface right in front of them.

Chapter 7

The roar around them was aggravated by the frenzied barking of all nine dogs. But Patrick was absolutely the leader of their pack. Even Mac, the lead dog, recognized it.

"Straight ahead!" Patrick shouted the command to the team.

Hoping he was making the right decision.

But they couldn't remain on the area of the ice where they were now. The crack was growing wider, longer. In moments, the part of the glacier where they stood would crash down into the water below.

Yet if this didn't work, they could sail into oblivion

as the huge ice chunk split off. Worse, they'd be crushed as it shifted while falling into the sea.

He couldn't help it. He reached down for Mariah, held her shoulder tightly in the same hand as he held the tugline, even as he grasped the handle bow in his other hand. To balance her, he told himself. Make sure she stayed steady.

Make sure *he* stayed steady.

The dogs leaped, beginning with Mac as sole lead dog, then one pair at a time, over the growing chasm, towing the sled behind them.

The noise of separating ice around them was deafening. For a second, they were airborne, Mariah and he, in the frail contraption that was the dogsled.

And then it landed on its runners and continued to plunge forward, towed by the heroic, unstoppable huskies.

Patrick breathed again—ignoring the sharp, tangy ozone scent still hanging in the cold air. He pulled gently on the tugline and yelled, "Whoa," attempting to be heard over the receding, but still loud, noises behind him. He repeated it as the dogs slowed but did not immediately stop.

And when they were completely halted, when good old Mac turned in his harness, ready to be praised for his excellent work—tongue out as though he were laughing—Patrick laughed, too.

He hurried around the sled, hugged Mac and the other dogs.

And then there was Mariah. She had maneuvered her way out of the sled.

He took her into his arms, feeling the thickness of her protective outer clothing, peeling away the scarf that obscured her beautiful face.

"We're okay," she breathed, smiling, her voice just loud enough to be heard over the cacophony still behind them.

"Yeah," he said, and lowered his mouth to hers.

How could she feel on fire in the middle of such a frigidly cold environment?

And how could she feel so safe after such a frightening near-death experience?

None of it had to make sense, Mariah knew. Not here, engulfed in Patrick's arms, with his lips, his tongue, his hands touching her in ways that made reality evaporate into a sensual celebration of life. And anticipation.

Their kiss was incredible. Although her mouth was the only part of her body that was truly warm, heat radiated from there, as if that one point of contact with Patrick's bare flesh was igniting her with an eternal flame.

But reality returned when a tremendous splash could be heard from the water far below. Mariah suddenly became aware again of their surroundings, their precarious situation. The dogs started barking anew. She pulled back, sad yet relieved as Patrick did the same.

Had only a few seconds passed? The sheered-off ice had apparently just hit the sea.

"We'd better move on." Patrick sounded almost as rueful as she felt. "But...hold that thought."

Smiling at him, she was rewarded with an answering grin so sexy that she once more regretted they weren't at a location where she could follow through with all that the kiss had suggested.

Only...as she turned to get back onto the sled, she remembered her real reason for being on the glacier. "Wait a minute," she told Patrick. She pulled her camera from her bag and, carefully, retraced the path the sled had taken them.

Back toward where the icy edge of the glacier had sheered off—not far from where they stood.

Mariah did not get very close to the edge as she took pictures. But she saw a huge iceberg floating in the middle of Tagoga Bay—a formation that had not been there before.

Oh, Lord. This time, using her telephoto setting, she snapped picture after picture of the sea life down below. Dead fish appeared on the surface. A few sea otters—dazed? Dead? No, they were mostly moving, albeit slowly. Dolphins in the distance blessedly swam away.

How, in this frigid environment, had the glacier calved so quickly, with no warning—except for the loud noise punctuated by the calls of killer whales she still hadn't seen? She'd also seen no indication of cracks in the surface, though there could have been a break below where they had been sledding and walking on the snowy face of the ice.

A shadow passed over them in the brilliance of the sunlight surrounding the area where they still stood. Several shadows. Mariah looked up to see three bald eagles soaring above, wings outstretched as if to take advantage of invisible yet powerful air currents. They were majestic, invincible, unfazed by the frightening experience that had just occurred below them.

And Mariah took full advantage by shooting their pictures, too—a tremendously uplifting contrast to the scattered, shattered creatures below.

When she was done, she couldn't help aiming the camera toward Patrick, who stood waiting at the rear of the sled. The dogs had assumed various positions of repose, and now looked unconcerned about the natural events that had resulted in their heroic leap over a potentially lethal void.

"Ready yet?" Patrick's tone was patient, but she could see, in the screen on her camera, that he appeared anything but. He was clearly ready to leave.

Perversely, she did not want to comply…entirely. And after their awful experience up here, she wanted to find more good things to remember and write about, not just the unnerving.

"Sure," she said. "Only…I know this was supposed to be a short excursion, but now that we're here I'd really love to head toward those peaks." She pointed inland to her left, over his shoulder. "I'm still hoping to see more wildlife up here. Get closer to a grizzly bear, maybe. Plus, those mountainsides just a little farther look like great places for Dall sheep to hang out. And, most of all, I still really want to try to find a wolf."

The wolf.

She peered over her camera, just in time to see the irritation on Patrick's face disappear into total—but intriguing—blankness.

"All right," he responded. "But I still don't want to stay out here very long." He gestured toward the seat on the sled. "Let's go."

The irony of it—maybe—was that there were indeed wolves in this area, Patrick thought as he got his dog team started over the ice in the direction Mariah had designated.

He'd spotted some in the distance often when

he came up here while in a similar form to them. Their pack mentality had caused them to edge in his direction, but he had discouraged them with growls and aggressiveness.

Wind whistled around the sled as he urged his team to even faster speeds, toward the ridges that no longer were so far away.

He was both irritated and impressed by Mariah's attitude. She'd gone through a scary, life-threatening situation and come out of it still filled with determination to accomplish her purpose.

He was ready to go back, though. He needed to record and send to the brass at Alpha Force all he'd seen, heard and smelled as the glacier had calved so violently and unexpectedly.

Some of those sensory phenomena had not seemed natural. Like last time.

Now, without Shaun to conduct online research on his behalf, he would have to do it himself. He had fortunately also brought a laptop computer but had only used it, since arriving here, to check email and send occasional messages to Drew Connell and other Alpha Force contacts.

Feeling a tug on his sleeve, he looked down. Mariah's beautiful face beamed, and she pointed off to their right. Had she spotted a creature she wanted to photograph?

He looked, and with his mind no longer focused

on his own musings, he also caught the scent: rabbit. No, here, it was snowshoe hares, white and nearly invisible against the snowy surface. Four were clustered around some sparse greenery thrusting up above the face of the ice.

"Whoa," he called to his team softly enough not to startle the wild creatures any more than necessary with the sound and sight of the dogsled. He utilized the tugline instead to keep the dogs' attention and slow them down.

When they stopped, not far from the wary creatures, Mariah smiled at him warmly as she uncurled herself from the sled and started taking pictures.

And when she was done, she touched his shoulder with her mittens and leaned up to kiss him with cold yet heatedly suggestive lips.

"Thanks," she said. "Now let's go back before we and the dogs freeze altogether. But thanks for your patience with me, Patrick. Those hares are lovely, and will make a wonderful addition to my article."

As they got back on the sled and headed toward the van, Patrick thought that it wasn't the hares around here that were lovely.

And he was definitely grateful that Mariah had apparently given up searching for any wolves today.

* * *

"This was all so amazing," Mariah told Patrick as they sat in the ranch house's kitchen, drinking hot chocolate.

The ride back had helped to warm her limbs and face, with the heat in the van on full blast, but her insides had yet to catch up.

"That glacier calving—my articles tend to be interesting, with a focus on local wildlife. I'm hesitant to include pictures of any suffering of the sea life we saw below, but it's part of what's going on here, and it's a direct result of whatever's happening to the glaciers. I'll have to consider that."

Patrick had not sat down at the table with her. Instead, he leaned on the counter near the sink, also drinking cocoa. "I'd suggest another meeting with Emil Charteris and his family, especially his son-in-law, to get his opinion on the effects you saw. Maybe you can just mention them in your story without incorporating the worst photos."

Interesting, Mariah thought. Patrick had zeroed in on pretty much the direction her thoughts had been heading. As if he gave a damn about the animals and her article.

She looked at him. She'd already, with no substantiation, gotten the impression that there was more to Patrick than an unambitious nomad who'd ended up here till the next time he decided to move on. If he was that same Patrick Worley she'd found online, he had even once been in the military.

But he obviously wasn't now. And assuming he was the drifter he appeared to be, it was only her hormones talking, insisting that she lust after the guy.

But she could still appreciate his insight...

"That's what I had in mind," she said. "Are you interested enough to join me when I get together with them next?"

"Why not?"

But she caught a fleeting expression that suggested his interest was a lot keener than his offhand comment.

Why?

When she got back to Inez's B and B around five that evening, Mariah called Emil Charteris and reached his voice mail. Next, she called Fiske's Hangout, and a harried-sounding Thea told her that Emil and his family had just walked in.

Mariah phoned Patrick. "Meet me at Fiske's in twenty minutes." She let him know that Emil and his gang were already there. She arrived first after a cold trek along sidewalks illuminated only by streetlights. The place didn't seem as crowded as usual, a potentially good thing for getting a discussion going.

The piano player was in the middle of pounding out a Billy Joel medley including "Piano Man."

Flynn Shulster sat at the table with Emil Charteris and his daughter and son-in-law. With the mouthy pseudoscientist spouting off, it might not be possible to direct the discussion the way she wanted. Nevertheless, Mariah had to try. She wended her way through what there was of the crowd and stood behind Jeremy Thaxton.

"Fairbanks," Shulster was saying. "That was where I shot my last documentary in Alaska, but it's nothing like the area around here, right on the water."

"Exactly what I hoped to talk about," Mariah interrupted. "I was on Afalati Glacier earlier today on a dogsled ride, and the darned thing calved right under us."

"Really?" Emil's head tilted as he seemed to notice her for the first time. "Have a seat and tell us about it." He stood, but Jeremy was faster and brought over a chair for Mariah.

"Patrick Worley is coming, too," she said. "He's the musher who took me on the glacier. I was out there researching my article and got some great wildlife photos of a grizzly bear, some snowshoe hares and bald eagles. But the creatures in the bay…" She shuddered. "I felt so bad for them. And the calving happened so suddenly."

"It sure did," Patrick said from behind her. He'd

brought his own chair over. "My job's potential longevity gets more limited every day. I'd really like an expert's opinion, Dr. Charteris, on what's causing the glaciers to come apart so violently and so fast."

Emil's expression grew annoyed. "Like I've said, I'm here to study it. I'll report my findings to the government, but right now I have no definitive answers even for them."

"When do you think you will?" Patrick's persistence only made Emil's frown deepen.

"And as *I've* said," Mariah interrupted, hoping to keep the others at the table from stomping off, "what I really want is an expert's opinion that I can quote about the effect on wildlife. Jeremy, here are the pictures I took." She leaned over in front of him and began scrolling through the photos on her digital camera. "Even if you can't comment specifically on the research you're doing, can't I at least get a general quote from you about the effect this kind of glacier calving causes to the sea life?"

"It's having a terrible effect," Flynn Shulster interjected. "And you may of course quote me. In fact, perhaps you and I should collaborate on studying the situation. Did you ever consider that the whole thing could be a government plot, and that's why they've given a grant to Dr. Charteris—to see if anyone can uncover the covert experiments being conducted by a top secret agency?"

"Don't be ridiculous, Flynn." Emil had stood at his seat and now glared at the TV scientist.

"Oh, I don't—" Mariah began, looking toward Patrick for help to counter this absurdity. But his expression suggested he found it interesting.

"Look, Mariah," Jeremy interrupted. "Maybe you should think about working with Flynn. I doubt you'll get anything but innuendoes and silliness for your article from him, but you know you can't get any genuine information from me, at least not now."

"Then you're not interested in getting copies of my pictures to draw your own conclusions. I had hopes we'd all cooperate with one another, at least to some extent."

A glance passed between Jeremy and Carrie, and then they both looked at Emil, who was seated again.

"Sorry, Mariah," he said. "I can't share information, and that goes for my staff, too."

"But not me," Flynn Shulster piped up with a broad smile.

"Fine, let's collaborate." She forced a smile as she stood up. "Sorry we couldn't work anything out, Emil. You might find my article very interesting when I'm done with it." She wasn't exactly happy with her attempt to get in a final dig and doubted that Emil or his family gave a damn about her irritation.

She had already ordered a meal, so she sat down

at another table. She was gratified when Patrick followed her, less so when Flynn also joined them.

"Sorry," she said with a sigh. "I shouldn't let my frustration show so much. But my nerves are still on edge after what we went through this afternoon."

"That does sound like a frightening experience," Flynn said. "I'd like to interview you both on my show. We'll do it in a few days, up there on the remaining part of the glacier. In exchange, I'll have my network send along other wildlife researchers who are willing to talk to you, okay?"

"As long as I can quote them in my article," Mariah said.

"Done."

But Patrick's frustration wasn't eased by their deal. He could have tried staying at the table with Emil Charteris but doubted he'd be welcome. And since the scientists weren't answering Mariah's questions, even with her substantial credentials as a writer, they certainly wouldn't answer a lowly musher's, especially because, to retain his cover, his inquiries couldn't get into much scientific detail.

As Carrie Thaxton approached the piano player—what was his name? Lemon?—and got him to play a loud rendition of "This Land Is Your Land," Patrick considered ordering another beer, then decided he shouldn't allow his frustration to ruin his better judgment.

Instead, he ate the sandwich he had already ordered and remained quiet. Listening…to nothing of much use to him.

What a farce of a day. Another bad calving on the glaciers that he'd experienced firsthand, without getting any more information on its cause. And no further leads about what happened to Shaun.

He'd hoped that his and Mariah's eyewitness description of this day's violent calving would at least raise Emil Charteris's interest enough to get him spouting theories. But that wasn't to be. So where could Patrick go with this now?

Most other scientists who'd been here conducting research had left the area, although some had indicated they would return. Sure, he could follow-up with them, but he needed immediacy. And depth.

And not innuendos about how the U.S. government was doing something to cause the situation that it wanted him to figure out.

But Flynn Shulster, the only one who appeared cooperative, was tossing out accusations without a shred of evidence. Well, no wonder. He might profess to be a scientist, but he was a showman.

Patrick identified with Mariah's frustration. And his was exacerbated by the fact that he, too, wanted answers but couldn't even let her know they had similar goals.

He had anticipated that his very special wolfen abilities would have already been of more help. Yet all he could do, at the moment, was to growl deep inside with frustration.

His mission here was to ask questions, to listen and utilize his other, keener senses. To learn—and to report back. His information was to lead to knowledge that would allow his superiors to determine who to send to fix whatever was going on.

His underlying skills as a medical doctor were irrelevant here, but he enjoyed the change.

He'd enjoy it even more once he had succeeded— even if that meant piggybacking on the curious Mariah's journalistic interrogations.

She had definitely impressed him with her courage on the ice today. He liked her. Was definitely attracted to her.

Even though he worried about her endless curiosity—when it appeared aimed toward him, and not solely in the directions that could lead to information he sought.

Under other circumstances, he might want to get to know her better. A lot better. Especially since she turned him on, even with her defiant scowl as she ate her meal of salmon and salad and discussed what would come next with Flynn.

But his lust for her could never be satisfied. He didn't dare get close to any woman while on a mission as vital and covert as this—especially not one who already asked too many questions.

Well, so what if he remained unsatisfied? He had other plans, at least for tonight.

He almost grinned when he recognized the song the piano player was banging out now—"Moondance" by Van Morrison. How appropriate.

Patrick would spend the night back up on the glacier.

Alone. And changed.

Chapter 8

Running on the ice, in the form he loved.

By choice again this night. But the full moon was coming. Soon. He would shift, then, no matter what he wanted.

Tonight's moonlight was invigorating. He could see as well as his human form did in daylight. By scent, he tracked and chased the hares he had seen earlier, for the sheer exhilaration of it.

But with no one to watch his back, he had drunk less elixir than usual. His time in wolf form was limited.

And he had work to do.

He quickly ended his chase. Turned toward what

was now the edge of the glacier. Stopped at the new, treacherous, broken rim of the ice.

Muzzle raised, he sniffed the air and listened.

The hint of ozone he had inhaled earlier had dissipated.

No call of orcas or crashes or any other sound besides the lapping of the bay below against the ice, the churning of the sea in the breeze.

Wait. The sounds. The lapping noise was something soft, yet insidious. Man-made. Was it the answer to what was happening here?

If not, it was at least a clue.

And somehow, he needed to figure it out.

"And you've no idea what it was?" demanded Major Drew Connell.

Patrick had called his commanding officer as soon as he'd returned to his apartment at the dogsled ranch. Which was a while after he'd first heard those noises in the water. He'd gone to a secluded area he'd been to before—one in a grove of barren trees, far enough from glaciers and the road to prevent him from being seen. There, he soon shifted back into human form, then returned to the ranch.

"No. Even though it resembled water hitting the side of something, I couldn't tell what it was or where it came from. Or even if that's what it was."

"You have a plan now to ID those noises?"

"Sure do. I'll work on it tomorrow."

* * *

But this wasn't the way he'd intended it, Patrick thought the next afternoon.

He had told Wes Dawes he needed part of the day off to help deal with some matters relating to Shaun's death—which just might be true.

Then he had come to the small dock area that served Tagoga Bay.

And had found he wasn't the only one with the idea of heading out into the waters that day. Mariah was there, too. She'd already chartered the vessel she had been on the first time she had seen a glacier calving here.

And had spotted him on the ice without knowing there was more to the wolf than a prowling canine.

Now they were on Nathan Kugan's boat together. It had just left the dock to sail toward Tagoga Bay and the glacier park. They both wore the same warm outerwear that they'd been bundled in yesterday, up on the ice. And needed it, since the wind was biting as the boat whipped through the water.

"So why did you decide to go out on a boat today?" Mariah asked suspiciously. Her hands were stuffed into her pockets, and her face, what was visible of it above her scarf, frowned—without marring its sexy loveliness.

"Just for fun." He turned to watch small waves at

the motorboat's side, holding the railing in his gloved hands.

"Of course," she responded sarcastically. "You know, Patrick, if you're following me, or—"

He interrupted her by laughing—though the idea of following her to someplace quiet and solitary, where they could be alone sent his imagination reeling in directions it shouldn't go. He controlled it. "No, really," he said. "I was as surprised about the coincidence as you. Or maybe it's not such a coincidence. Okay, I'll level with you. I was freaked out yesterday when that glacier broke apart with us on it. I wanted to take a look from the water, and hiring someone like Nathan to take me seemed like a good idea. I assume you're here for the same reason, although I figure you'll write about it, too."

She nodded. "That's pretty much it. Plus, I wanted to see the sea creatures there now. Find out if at least some are okay and get a few photos."

The boat started turning into Tagoga Bay, and she stopped speaking as the sheer, icy cliff faces came into view.

"Breathtaking," she whispered.

He looked at her. "Yeah." Then he grinned as she turned and glared at him. "The glacier park," he said.

A short while later, they stopped in the middle of the bay and were soon joined on the deck by Captain

Nathan Kugan. Patrick had met the guy before at Fiske's. Nathan was a relatively short guy, middle-aged or more, with weathered, swarthy skin and a look of the native Aleutians about him.

"You were at Afalati Glacier when it calved yesterday?" he asked.

"Yes." Mariah pointed toward a distant glacier on the port side. "That one, right?"

Patrick nodded as Nathan said, "Yep. Know what Afalati means in Inupiaq—that's a language dialect of the Inuit?"

"No," Mariah said, and Patrick could see how fascinated the writer had suddenly become. "What?"

"Governor. If you want, I'll print you a sheet from the internet that gives the names of this park's glaciers and their origins."

"I'd love it!" Her enthusiasm made Patrick grin—though he knew he shouldn't let anything about Mariah appeal to him so much. They weren't enemies, of course, but neither could they be friends… or more.

Just imagine what she could do to him—and Alpha Force—if she ever learned the truth and decided to write it up for her damned magazine.

"And another thing," Nathan said. "By the articles you've written for *Alaskan Nature,* I gather that you've been in Alaska for more than a year, so that makes you a Sourdough, but Patrick hasn't been here for one of our fine winters yet, so he's considered a Cheechako."

Mariah laughed as she made notes, and Patrick couldn't help grinning at her. "I'll try to use that in my upcoming article," she said.

"So…I'd imagine that fellow is the result of the calving you saw yesterday." Nathan pointed toward the far starboard side of his boat. The large chunk of ice there was so huge, and so close to the nearest glaciers, that Patrick hadn't noticed at first that it wasn't part of them.

"Could be," Mariah breathed.

"Well, damn," Nathan said. "That's one of the biggest bergs I've seen broken off lately. And what do you want to bet it'll eventually escape from this bay and get out in the gulf? And endanger not only my boat, but bigger ones like cruise ships and oil tankers. Whatever's going on here—I don't like it."

"It's only been a few days since I asked you the last time," Mariah said, "but do you or any of the other captains have additional ideas about what's causing this? And, of course, its effects on the local wildlife?"

"Nothing different from what I told you before," he said. "Though we've seen a lot more dead fish floating on the water."

"After our experience yesterday, I'm interested, too." Patrick took a step closer to the captain. Any bit of additional knowledge he gathered, no matter what the source, could only help fulfill this Alpha Force assignment—and his ideas of where to look for answers certainly needed more stimulation.

But Nathan's theories were basically the same old global-warming stuff, nothing helpful to explain the extent and immediacy of the decimation.

"Can we get any closer to Afalati?" Patrick soon asked.

"Sure thing."

Nathan returned to the bridge of his small ship and they started moving again. When they stopped, the glacier where Patrick and Mariah had been yesterday loomed before them, tall and frigid and imposing.

And silent. Once their boat's motors were stopped, Patrick heard nothing beyond normal—breaking of small waves against the craft and ice, calls of distant birds and barks of sea lions.

Nothing that resembled the quiet lapping noises of last night that had so intrigued and worried him.

"Beautiful," Mariah said beside him, "but I don't see any wildlife either up there or in the water today. Certainly no wolves." She sounded disappointed, which filled Patrick with all sorts of conflicting emotions. If she only knew…

"I guess I've seen enough for today, Nathan. If Patrick's ready, could you just take us back to the dock?"

A while later, Mariah stood in the small, open parking lot near the marina with Patrick. It had been treated with salt, and its surface was slushy, but she enjoyed its view of the mostly empty docks and the rough surface of the wind-tossed water.

She was impressed that Patrick had offered to pay half the charge for the boat rental. He probably didn't have much money, as a musher, and she was on a small but handy expense account.

He had joined her in thanking Nathan for their outing but had remained quiet since their stop at the base of Afalati Glacier.

"This outing was definitely enjoyable," she said as they approached his car, "but I'd hoped to learn more about why we experienced such a violent calving yesterday."

He shrugged a broad shoulder beneath his jacket and tossed her an ironic smile. "Global warming." He pulled his right hand from the pocket of his jeans. His car key dangled from it.

"It's got to be more than that." She knew she sounded almost belligerent.

"Could be. Anyway, see you around, Mariah." And then he slid into his car.

He didn't drive off, though, until she had gotten into her SUV, started the engine, and pulled out of her parking spot—gentlemanly, despite his subliminal message: he had no interest in seeing her later today.

Which irritated her. She had sensed vibes between them. More. A definite sexual attraction.

One he had no interest in following up on, notwithstanding what she might want.

Well, okay. After the way her last relationship had ended, she'd been reluctant to get involved with anyone, so why start now? But she wanted to go back out on the glaciers at least one more time. Maybe it would help to have someone besides Patrick be her guide, for a different perspective.

In any event, she'd have to go to Great Glaciers Dogsled Ranch to set it up. She would do it that afternoon. She would also ask the Daweses if either had an opinion on the glacier calving, and, more important, what kind of wildlife they typically saw while on the ice these days, and whether it used to be different.

Wolves, maybe, like the one that had so captured her attention and imagination.

Toby had been in business for a while. His perspective would be interesting. Possibly even quotable for her article.

She smiled as she pulled her vehicle onto the

two-lane road toward downtown. At least she had a plan.

And if she happened to see Patrick there, well, so what?

Once again, when Mariah arrived at the ranch, a lot of huskies played noisily in the fenced-in yard to the side of the driveway. Not as many as she'd seen there before, though. Some were probably out on dogsled outings.

She whipped out her camera and took a few photos. Maybe she would do another story, one strictly devoted to dogsledding. That might have a lot of appeal to *Alaskan Nature Magazine* readers, especially those from the lower forty-eight who had never been out mushing.

Mariah continued up the driveway toward the main house. No Patrick in her path this time. No one else came out to greet her, either.

This could be an opportunity. She veered along the side of the driveway, passed by the main house and headed toward the back building that she'd been told contained the employees' apartments.

The place where Patrick had found Shaun Bethune's body.

Because she was interested in learning the truth, she had agreed with her boss, Harold, and would attempt to find out enough to do an article on it for one of his other publications. This could be a good time to do a little research.

"Hey," called a familiar voice from behind her. She turned to see Patrick emerge from the far side of the main house. A large dog followed him—his dog Duke, wasn't it? Interestingly, they both had eyes in amberlike shades of brown. Well, people were always said to choose dogs that resembled them.

"Hi," she called with false cheeriness. Busted. She headed toward him. "I'm here to schedule my next dogsled ride. And I'd also like to talk to one of the Daweses, preferably Toby, about his take on local wildlife."

"You didn't mention either this morning." Patrick's tone was mild, but his scowl made her feel defensive. Duke sat down on the icy walk beside him.

"I didn't think about either this morning." Not exactly the truth.

"Well, you should have called first. Both Toby and Wes are out giving tours. The other guys, too."

She was alone with Patrick? She felt suddenly warm, and it had nothing to do with what she was wearing. She looked into Patrick's eyes and saw his awareness there, too—hot and lusty.

"Any idea how long they'll be?"

"None. But I'll tell them you were here."

Well, hell. He wanted her to leave. Which made her, perversely, want to dig in her heels.

Maybe she could even seduce him, to encourage his apparent interest so she could learn something about Shaun's death and make Harold happy....

Too bad that wasn't her. Although the idea of having sex with him just for the fun of it had more appeal than she wanted to admit to herself.

She decided to hang around a little longer if possible—not for seduction, but to see what information about Shaun she could extract from Patrick.

"Any chance of getting a cup of hot chocolate?" she asked. "I'm cold!" She gave a little shiver in punctuation.

"If you got back in your car and turned on the heater on your way to town, you'd warm up."

"You're right, but it would feel a whole lot better if I had a nice warm drink first."

"Okay." His curtness didn't sound as if he'd decided yet to let her stay long. "But it'll have to be a short one. I've got work to do. And not in the main house—it's locked up right now."

Mariah would get to see at least part of the building where Patrick lived...and Shaun died. Trailed by Duke, Patrick ushered her along the driveway and into the back building, then into a first-floor kitchen smaller and more sparsely furnished than the one in the main house. He grabbed a pot and put water on the stove to boil.

"So this is where you stay?" she asked. She stood near the sink, looking through the window behind it toward woods filled with bleak, leafless trees.

"That's right."

He obviously wasn't about to keep up a conversation, so it was up to her. "And your friend Shaun—where was his apartment?"

"Upstairs."

"Yours, too?"

"Near his." Turning his back, he took some white mugs from a wood-fronted cabinet on the wall beside the sink.

This was becoming more than irritating. But she wasn't about to give up.

She waited while he poured boiling water over the cocoa mix in their cups, then stirred in some tiny marshmallows. He handed her a mug and his hand brushed hers. He felt it, too, and stared down at the contact with a sensuality in his gaze that made her shiver.

Licking her lips suggestively, she tasted the brew. Good, hot and sweet. But she really had no appetite for it.

She put the mug back down on the laminated counter with a thump that startled the dog, who'd been asleep on the floor. Patrick turned his back, looking out the window. "Okay," she said finally.

"I've got some questions for you, Patrick. About your secrets."

He turned, his expression blank—and she missed his earlier heated gaze. "What secrets?"

"You tell me. What don't you want me to know? You only ask questions, never answer anything directly. I don't think you killed your friend Shaun— from what I can tell, you're genuinely grieving over him. But there's something else. I'm sure of it. And I'm not going to give up until you tell me what—"

Suddenly, his mug was beside hers on the counter. He grabbed her, pulled her tightly against him, and shut her up—by lowering his mouth firmly onto hers.

She resisted only for an instant, then threw herself into the kiss. Was this what she'd wanted all along?

One of his hands held her so firmly against him that she felt his hardness, pushed herself even closer. His other hand stroked her back, her buttocks. She moaned as it moved forward to cup one breast, tease her nipple…

"You want to know my secrets?" he rasped against her mouth. "Then come upstairs with me, Mariah."

What could she do but comply?

Bad idea, Patrick cautioned himself. But he nevertheless held Mariah close to his side as they stumbled up the stairs. At the top of the steps, he kissed her again, hard, glad that no one else was around that day. Or maybe that wasn't such a good thing.

It made it so much easier for him to commit this foolish—yet inevitable—act.

"Last chance to leave," he muttered against her mouth.

"No way," she breathed.

And then they were inside the box that was his apartment. He closed the door to keep out Duke, who'd followed them. He saw Mariah glance around, probably noting its tininess, its sparseness—then thrust herself back against him.

Damn, but she got to him. Turned him on so he didn't wait even to reach the bed. Her spicy scent intoxicated him, surging through his blood stream, making him want even more—of it, of her. A hallucinogen? Addictive? Hell, yes.

She'd left her jacket downstairs. Good. One less obstruction. He pulled at the hem of her green sweater, yanking it over her head. And then he had her pants off, touching her everywhere. Wanting more. Kissing her smooth, hot skin.

"Now, Patrick," she gasped as she tugged at his own sweater. "Please."

Whatever the rest of Patrick's secrets, one was that he was the sexiest man imaginable under his cool, aloof demeanor and his warm Alaskan clothes.

And suddenly, exhilaratingly, that was a secret no longer. Mariah was in his bed. Beneath him as his hands and mouth caressed her until every inch of her was alert, on fire. Needing more.

Needing him.

And yet, despite his own obvious need, he pulled away—and she soon heard a crackle of plastic that told her he had maintained some degree of awareness and sanity, perhaps better than she had. But she reached down, determined to participate, to sheathe him with the condom.

And then, at last, he was inside her. Moving, bucking, causing her to react in unison with him, meeting his thrusts. More, and harder, and—she finally screamed his name, even as he, too, cried out.

Slowly, slowly, her breathing settled down. She turned into him, clasped in his strong arms as he, too, caught his breath. Warmed by a body she could only term as phenomenal.

But as her awareness returned, so did her consciousness. She may have experienced the best sex in her life, the best sex imaginable.

But she still had not learned any of Patrick Worley's secrets.

Chapter 9

Gentleman that he was, Patrick had allowed Mariah to shower first in his apartment's small bathroom. Alone. He'd initially expressed concern that others might return soon to the building. Although two of them showering together could theoretically save time, chances were that they'd wind up back in bed. Against the wall. On the floor. Making love all over again.

The thought made Mariah shiver deliciously, even now.

But as Patrick showered, she used the time alone to put her clothes on and repair her hair and makeup as well as possible, considering that she had left her tote bag and its contents downstairs.

She let Duke into the apartment and made a fuss over him. The poor dog had started making noises out in the hall, where Patrick had exiled him.

Giving Duke a reassuring hug, Mariah stood and looked into the mirror attached to the small dresser. She'd have done better with some lip gloss, but she had found a comb of Patrick's so her hair wasn't too awful.

A phone rang nearby, from somewhere in the apartment. Mariah looked around. Should she notify Patrick to come out and answer? He probably had voice mail. Even so, she looked for the phone, then realized that the ring emanated from the large backpack she'd seen Patrick carry on the night he had spent at Inez's.

The night he had found poor Shaun…

Shaun! She'd gotten so distracted that she had forgotten what a great opportunity she had, being inside the building where he had been killed.

Maybe she could duck into the apartment that had been his and look around.

But first, she should check the caller ID on the still-ringing phone so she could at least let Patrick know who it was.

Kneeling by the backpack, where it lay on the floor beside the dresser, she unzipped it and reached in—just as the phone stopped ringing. Oh, well. She started to withdraw her hand, but felt something odd. She pulled the pack open farther.

Looking inside, she saw a cloth bag that contained something that felt…well, smooth. She was curious, but left it alone when she noticed a large, opaque bottle. Booze of some kind? Odd, that Patrick would carry alcohol. She'd gotten the impression at Fiske's that his beer consumption was pretty light, and she'd not seen him with anything stronger.

Curious, she pulled the bottle out—and saw that its label was not a commercial distributor's but what appeared to be a prescription with no identification of the drug inside. It had Patrick's name on it, though, with directions "Take as needed."

Strange. Was Patrick ill? Was that why he was so secretive? He certainly didn't act as if anything was wrong, but who knew?

Of course, this could simply be a health supplement or vitamins, although why would they be prescribed for him?

Or…if Patrick was the guy she'd found on the internet, who was once with the U.S. military and then discharged under less than honorable circumstances, could it have been for using drugs—like this? If so, what was it?

Well, it wasn't really her concern. Having sex, no

matter how extraordinary it had been, didn't give her any say in how he lived his life.

But she'd nevertheless try to find a subtle way to ask him.

"What the hell are you doing?"

She turned to see Patrick standing in the bathroom doorway, wrapped only in a towel tied at his waist. She couldn't help staring, smiling in sexual awareness... until she caught his expression.

Fury raged on his face, furling his pale brown eyebrows and jutting his lower jaw. He crossed the room and yanked the bottle from her grip.

"I...your cell phone was ringing, and I thought I'd hand it to you." She hated how defensive she sounded.

"Thanks," he said curtly. "Now, I think it's time for you to leave."

She rose to her full height and glared at him. "I agree," she said coldly. "But I'd like to know if you're ill, Patrick. It's a reasonable question for me to ask, considering that we just made love. Does that bottle contain prescription medicine?"

Of course he had used a condom. So even if he was on meds for some sexually transmitted disease, he had kept her safe.

"It's. Not. Your. Business." He accentuated each word menacingly.

"I suppose not." She turned and strode toward the door. Duke stayed by her side, and she stopped just long enough to pat the large, furry dog. And then she turned back to Patrick and spoke softly, as if they were parting as friends. "You look good to me, Patrick. I'll assume you're not ill. But if you are—or if you're on something you shouldn't be—and you need help, you know where to find me."

She left the apartment and closed the door behind her, leaving Duke inside.

And stood still in the narrow hallway, energy spent.

Damn Patrick and his secrets! Why didn't he just explain the bottle, without putting her on the defensive?

She started to leave—then noticed the police tape cordoning off a door farther down the hall.

That had to be Shaun's apartment.

She went to that door and stopped. There was enough tape on it that she couldn't easily get by. The door was most likely locked.

Even if she could get inside, she doubted she'd see any clues the cops hadn't picked up.

But then it hit her.

What if Shaun's murder had something to do with Patrick's secret...wrapped up in that mysterious bottle?

"Damn!" Patrick wanted to ram his fist into the apartment wall, but breaking his hand wouldn't solve anything.

Duke, on the floor beside him, stared up with nervous bug eyes.

"I could just have laughed it off. Told her it was some dumb homeopathic stuff I take to build my muscles. Whatever."

What made it even worse was that Patrick had anticipated…something. Mariah was a writer. Filled with curiosity. Even if it was focused on wildlife, that wasn't all she was interested in.

But he'd been taken off guard by the truly excellent sex they'd just shared. Had even started wondering, just a little, about where this might go.

How much she could learn about him before she'd run off screaming. Or start asking more questions for some damned magazine article.

Now he'd have to fix this—somehow. See Mariah again, explain his embarrassment that she'd found his stupid indulgence, laugh it off.

And then not see her again. Ever.

Not touch that mind-blowing body of hers…

He stalked across the room. Picked up his backpack. Looked inside—and confirmed that the elixir and light were still there. At least she hadn't sneaked out with them.

He dug down again and extracted his cell phone, the supposed origin of all this trouble. When he looked at it, he saw he had, in fact, missed a call, from Drew Connell.

Taking a deep breath, he sat down at his kitchen table and called his superior officer back.

"No further leads on what happened to Shaun yet," Patrick responded to Drew's inquiry. "I've got a few more ideas, though."

He had, of course, checked the other mushers' rooms and found no evidence that any had harmed Shaun—and also found no laptop. But he'd discovered that Pilke of the local police liked to brag a bit, so he was working on grabbing a beer with him to learn if there was anything on the official's radar. But so far Pilke had remained unavailable.

"Keep at it," Drew said, then paused. "You okay? You sound…ragged."

"Nothing I can't deal with," Patrick shot back, then said, "Sorry. I came a little close to being outed by a magazine writer who's too nosy for her own good."

"Be careful," Drew said. "I'd send you more help, but we've had all members of the team involved in that mine sabotage matter I told you about. It doesn't help that I get frequent calls from General Yarrow. He's receiving pressure from on high because the whole mining industry, including a mega-mogul who speaks for all of them—Austin DiLisio—is making lots of angry noise about getting results. Fast."

"Want me to come back and help?" He had to suggest it, though the idea tore Patrick in many directions. He'd be leaving a mission without completing it. He'd be running out on Shaun, without finding who'd murdered him.

And—hell, he admitted it to himself. He didn't like leaving Mariah. And not just because he figured she wouldn't accept his explanation of the elixir.

"No, I talked it over with the general. The higher-ups are watching what you're doing, too. The destruction in the Arctic Ocean and other ice shelves have seemed more comprehensible. What's happening in your part of Alaska needs better explanation before we bring you back and send someone with whatever skills you find are needed to fix it. So…when will you have some answers?"

"Soon," Patrick promised.

And hoped he wasn't lying to his commanding officer.

Mariah headed for the Tagoga Police Station. At least this way, she could tell Harold she had tried to research the extra story he wanted, the one about Shaun's murder.

The Tagoga P.D. was in one of the two modern hexagonal-shaped buildings in the town's civic center. Detective Gray, in charge of Shaun's case, agreed to talk to her, but he didn't say much. He was a tall, older guy with gray sideburns that ended in muttonchops framing his mouth, who mostly frowned and said the case was still under investigation so he couldn't talk about it to the media. He rolled his eyes when she gave him her business card identifying her as a magazine writer.

So what now? Coming here had also been one way to keep her mind off what it really wanted to focus on: Patrick. Hot sex. And medicines and secrets.

She needed to focus on her wildlife story. Get enough info to write it and leave here, no matter how hard that might be. What she had gotten from the high school teacher was a good start. Jeremy Thaxton wasn't about to cooperate with her, and there didn't seem to be other authorities on wildlife present in Tagoga just now except for Flynn Shulster, if she could even count him.

Well, if she had to she would just go with the celebrity angle. People might even pick up copies of the magazine to get the opinion of a TV personality like Shulster.

Time to schedule an interview.

Mariah covered her yawn as she sat at the table with Flynn Shulster and his hangers-on. It didn't help that the piano player was into lethargic middle-of-the-road oldies tonight.

When Flynn stopped talking after what felt like an hour, she asked, "So you'll meet with me tomorrow for an interview on your opinions about global warming, and what impact you've seen on animals?"

"Of course." He winked at her. "We know there's a lot more to it, don't we?" The crowd around him cheered.

Mariah needed a break. She excused herself to head toward the restroom.

Which was when Patrick Worley entered with Toby and Wes Dawes and others from the Great Glaciers Dogsled Ranch.

She couldn't avoid him—not when the others greeted her so effusively. And so she said hello. And tried not to think about the magnificent male body hidden under the navy sweater and slacks and his unzipped jacket.

"Hello, Mariah." His low voice sent a shiver of desire creeping up her back.

He might be on drugs, she reminded herself.

Or be ill…

Well, she might be worried about him, but he clearly didn't want her concern.

She took her time in the restroom, trying to get her thoughts in order. She would interview Flynn Shulster tomorrow.

And maybe she would leave Tagoga earlier than she had intended, use what she had gotten so far to write a puff piece rather than the substantive article she had hoped for.

She wouldn't have to torture herself by seeing Patrick anymore. Remembering the delights they had so briefly shared. And wondering about that unidentified stuff he didn't want to talk about.

She swiped her comb through her hair once more and headed back into the bar/restaurant. And looked around. Patrick and the Daweses had taken Flynn Shulster's table, and he had moved to one right next to it—without his bunch of fans but with Emil Charteris and his family.

Maybe this was an opportunity.

She wasn't surprised when Emil, Jeremy and Carrie gave her brief but not particularly welcoming greetings. Flynn, on the other hand, appeared glad to see her again.

"You really ought to take Mariah on your submarine one of these days, Emil," Flynn said as he stood to pull out a chair for Mariah. "You're interested in underwater creatures, too, aren't you, Mariah?"

"Sure," she said, puzzled. "Submarine?"

"As part of studying the chaotic glacier calving around here, Emil and his team rented a mini-sub to take in the action and effects underwater. What have you seen so far?" he asked, looking back at Emil. "And when will you come on my program and let me interview you about it?"

"How did you—? Well, never mind. Yes, I did rent a small submersible as part of my ongoing research here." Emil looked disgruntled, as if he was admitting to a big secret.

Mariah glanced over at Patrick. He was looking at Emil, too.

Emil continued, "I wanted to have it available in case I needed to examine something underwater. With the water as deep and cold as it is around here, I didn't want to rely on diving. But I haven't used it much more than to try it out. Now tell me how you knew about it." He glared at Flynn.

"I rented a boat of my own—a regular little motor job—and found myself in the vicinity of your camp. I saw the pontoon transport craft holding the sub out of the water, that's all. So…when will you take us for a ride?" Flynn looked at Mariah and winked.

"Forget it," Emil grumbled.

At the same time, his daughter smiled at Flynn. "It is a lot of fun on one of those things," Carrie admitted. "But, you know, Dad's paying for it out of his government research grant. There are restrictions and limitations on liability and all that good stuff. As much as we'd like to use it for entertaining, we really can't."

Mariah glanced toward Jeremy Thaxton. Was he okay with the way his wife seemed to be playing up to the TV personality? Apparently so, since he was nodding in her direction.

"We get it, don't we, Flynn?" Mariah said. "But

if that ever changes, please let us know. I'd love a minisub view of local sea life. Not to mention your commentary on it, Jeremy." She aimed a hopeful grin in the zoologist's direction, but he just looked away.

Mariah soon said good-night and started walking toward the door.

Why wasn't she surprised to find Patrick outside in the brisk Alaskan air with her?

"Lovely night," she said noncommittally. What she wanted to ask was how the beer she'd seen him nursing went with the stuff in the bottle. Even more than that, she wanted to ask if he was well, how he was feeling.

Most of all, she wanted to throw herself into his arms and kiss those amazing lips…one last time.

She did none of it.

"Yeah, it is," Patrick said. And then he turned and walked away.

Chapter 10

It was very early in the morning when Patrick got out of his car and headed inside toward his apartment. Security lights were the only illumination. No one else appeared to be awake, and not even Duke was barking.

Patrick had prowled a new portion of the glacier park that night, one he hadn't been to in wolf form before. He'd heard and scented nothing out of the ordinary. Maybe he should have stayed at Fiske's Hangout.

Earlier, being near the table where Mariah was seated had been a plus in more ways than one. He had been able to watch her without it being too obvious.

Seen her for what might wind up being the last time. A good thing.

Why didn't he feel better about it?

At least he'd been able to eavesdrop. If the sounds he'd heard before belonged to the submarine Emil Charteris hired, then the scientist had been lying about how frequently he was using it—which suggested that his reason for using it was different, as well.

Something potentially interesting to follow-up on. But not tonight. Or tomorrow night, either, when his shifting would be beyond his control.

He opened his door and flicked on the lights, kneeling to accept Duke's effervescent greeting. His eyes immediately gravitated toward the bed in his small studio apartment. He thought about that afternoon, and what he had shared here with Mariah. With regret? Yeah—that it wouldn't happen again.

He locked the door. Hefting the strap off his shoulder, he put down his backpack on the small table near the kitchen area. The elixir and light inside had functioned as intended this evening.

And had aroused too many questions in Mariah's curious mind that afternoon.

She had assumed he was ill—or on some kind of illegal drugs. Logical stuff, for a logical kind of human.

Maybe she'd looked him up on the internet,

found a Patrick Worley who'd been dishonorably discharged from the military—the cover story that had been planted about him. Though not all sources mentioned it, the reason had allegedly been for drug use. Mariah might jump to that conclusion anyway, thanks to what she'd found in his knapsack. And if so, she would undoubtedly stay far away from him now if she thought he had a habit he hadn't kicked.

Had she learned that the same Patrick Worley had grown up in an area filled with werewolf legends?

What would she really think if she knew what the things she had found were used for? She had asserted a particular interest in wolves, in her wildlife predilection.

Good thing he planned to be way off on the farthest of the glaciers tomorrow night. Nowhere near Mariah and her assumptions about him and his addictions.

Or whatever else she thought about him.

What a mistake, Mariah thought the next day as she walked into Elegance, Tagoga's one and only high-end restaurant, with Flynn.

She had suggested meeting him at Fiske's. But when she had called him this morning to confirm their interview, he had made it clear that he intended to hold court with her here.

At her expense.

For the sake of her article, she had agreed. And hoped that she at least got something quotable from him.

The place wasn't very busy. It smelled of luscious gourmet foods—exotic herbs and spices. "Let's sit there." Flynn pointed to a table for two near a window. The tablecloth was a pristine white, set with ornate silverware. Mariah felt gratified when Flynn asked only for hot tea to drink, instead of an expensive wine to fill one of the goblets at their table.

After the server had taken their drink orders, Mariah said, "So what's your opinion on wildlife in Tagoga? Abundant or not?"

She put her recorder on the table, and poised her pen over the tablet she'd brought to take notes.

Flynn began pontificating on how great it was to visit Alaska and see wonderful creatures such as bald eagles, coyotes, Arctic foxes, wolves, lynxes, voles, shrews and weasels—but not all around Tagoga.

"Which have you spotted locally?"

His response wasn't surprising: basically a re-iteration of the animals Mariah had seen.

"Have you taken any pictures?" she asked Flynn.

"Of course. Film clips I can use on my show, with commentary. I'll let you see them, but if you want to use any in your article you'll need to buy the right."

That figured. "I'll have enough of my own," she said, loathe to commit to spend more money than she had to on Flynn Shulster—especially when he ordered an expensive steak sandwich for lunch—even in the interest of maintaining collegiality. She stuck with soup and a small salad.

When their order had been taken, Mariah skimmed her notes on what she planned to ask Flynn. But before she got into more interview questions, he said, "You've been out on the glaciers a lot, haven't you?"

"A bit, yes. I'm hoping to focus my article on wildlife on the ice."

"Are you going to include sled dogs in your article, too? I heard you've been going out often with that musher Patrick—and not just on the glaciers."

Mariah felt herself redden. "He's been a helpful resource," she responded cautiously.

"Well, watch out for him. You know he was a friend of that fellow Shaun, who got murdered, right?"

She needed to get the interview back on track. "Yes. Now, how about you—do you believe going out on dogsleds gives any greater access to wildlife, or less?"

"No other animal's going to want to get close to a bunch of running dogs all trying to be alpha. You know, neither Patrick nor Shaun had been here very long before the murder, so who else could have been mad enough at Shaun to kill him?"

Not a bad question, perhaps. But not one she wanted to get into with Flynn. "Let's leave that to the local authorities." Wanting an excuse to get away from Flynn for a few minutes to reconsider her approach, Mariah glanced around. Oh, yes, the usual means of escape—she noticed a discreet sign for the restroom. She also noticed that Jeremy Thaxton sat alone at a table at the far side of the room.

"Excuse me," she said and stood. On her way to the restroom, she made a brief stop at Jeremy's table. "Hi," she said. "Is Carrie here with you?"

She was on a restroom break, too.

"My discussion with Flynn is fascinating," she lied, "but I'd love your take on what he has been telling me. May I schedule you for an interview just to talk about that?" Not that she really expected a positive answer.

"Sorry." He peered up at her through his glasses. "We've made it clear that we can't talk about our work, even peripherally."

Mariah nodded ruefully. "If that ever changes, please let me know." She headed for the ladies' room.

Hearing a low voice, she turned the corner at the end of the hall. Carrie Thaxton's back was toward her, and she held up a cell phone to her ear.

Despairing of Jeremy's cooperation, Mariah decided to press her case with Carrie, once she was off the phone. But Mariah's attention was immediately captured by Carrie's whisper. "Kaley Glacier? Tonight? Another calving—major breakage?"

Was she talking to her dad? But what had Emil Charteris found out? And how did he know there would be more damage tonight?

Mariah was sure Carrie wouldn't tell her, and she didn't want to reveal she had been listening in.

But Mariah suddenly knew where she would be that night.

Coming by dogsled would have been much easier, Mariah thought as she slid on rented skis across the icy surface of Kaley Glacier. Still, she loved cross-country skiing, and the opportunity of indulging in it on the glacier felt exhilarating—even though, this time, she had a reason besides the fun of it.

She had driven to the glacier park and parked her SUV as close to her goal as possible.

She'd contacted Toby Dawes at Great Glaciers Dogsled Ranch first, told him she wanted someone to take her out on Kaley Glacier that evening—preferably not Patrick, although she said nothing critical about him.

But no one was available—not even Patrick, who had taken the day off.

She had started out late in the afternoon. At least it was still daylight now. She wasn't sure how long she would have to remain near the edge of Kaley Glacier before the calving Carrie had described on the phone might occur—or not. If it did, she hoped it would be early, but at least she should be able to see any changes even late, under the light of tonight's full moon.

She had bundled up in layers, including a thick knit cap and matching scarf to protect her face. And battery-operated socks and hand warmers.

It was quiet out here. All she heard was the whooshing of her skis on the glacier's surface.

She was delighted to glimpse some small, furry white animals darting around not too far from her. She stopped, pulled her camera out of her bag and used the telephoto lens to snap pictures of the Arctic foxes.

But where was the wolf?

She also saw a few gull-like white-and-gray kittiwakes fly by overhead. But if it weren't for the blueness of the nearly cloud-free sky, she might think that the entire world had morphed entirely into multiple shades of white.

Fortunately, even sliding this fast, she wasn't especially cold. She only hoped she'd be able to stand the chill long enough once she reached her goal. If not, she would leave. At least she had brought enough gear, as she always did on research trips into less populated areas of Alaska, including a powerful battery-operated light, a cell phone and an iridium satellite phone she'd rented in advance. Its GPS would ensure she could always find her way back.

At one point she saw a grizzly bear in the distance and shot its photo, too. And then she kept going. Until she reached the area near the edge of Kaley Glacier.

Not too close, though. Having had such a close call before, when the glacier she was on had calved, she didn't want to experience anything like that again.

She stopped some distance from the ice's end, looked around and saw nothing out of the ordinary. The mounds of ice and snow suggested that the recent calving had sheered off the most sedate part of the glacier's surface. She stood, staring down as best she could into the ice-mottled water far below.

What was she looking for?

Hell if she knew. But daylight was starting to fade. Carrie's overheard comment hadn't specified a time for the supposed major breakage to occur, only that it would be tonight.

Maybe. There were certainly no guarantees that anything would happen on Kaley Glacier tonight.

Not even the appearance of that elusive wolf, darn it.

As Mariah continued scanning the water from this

distance, she thought she heard a deep crash from somewhere below her, but only for a moment.

It was followed by the frantic call of a pod of orcas.

Which was when she heard a violent cracking noise and the ground started to tremble.

Damn the woman! Patrick thought, sliding across the ice on cross-country skis. He hadn't dared bring any of the dogs along this night, not even Duke. But at the town's main rental store, he had confirmed that Mariah had rented similar skis earlier that afternoon.

Patrick had gotten word from Toby that Mariah had contacted him about hiring a dog team to go to Kaley Glacier that day. She hadn't said why but had made it clear that she would go on her own if no one could take her.

Of course Patrick couldn't take her today—not with tonight's fast-approaching full moon. But he didn't like the idea of her going out on the ice by herself. Especially because Toby had the impression that she expected something to occur there that evening.

One way or another, she could be putting herself in danger, and he needed to find her in time and convince her—fast—to go back. Not that he harbored much hope she'd listen to him. But he'd just have to find a way to scare her into returning, if necessary.

It might not be hard to convince her that he was stalking her, if he just happened to show up in the middle of nowhere, exactly where she was heading. But he'd better find her quickly—or he'd have to give up on the idea of trying to save her. Daylight was already starting to wane.

At least she had mentioned Kaley Glacier, but as he drew closer to the water side, the ice field's rises and crags seemed to multiply. He couldn't see the edge.

He slowed down, moved more carefully now. Looked around, and listened.

He stopped skiing as he detected a scent in the air. Ozone?

What—

And then came the sounds he'd heard before—an explosion. Orcas. Cracking—

He heard a scream.

Mariah frantically attempted to shove herself, on her skis, even farther inland. The sun, now just above the horizon, created a huge, orange glow that lit up the ice around her, making it even harder for her to see where to head.

The ground's shaking below her accelerated, like an earth tremor she had once experienced in

California, only a whole lot fiercer. Worse, even, than the last glacier calving she had experienced here.

Damn! How many could she go through and still survive?

Would she survive?

And why was she experiencing this again?

A huge crack appeared to her left. The vast section of ice she was on started separating from the rest.

She screamed again, trying frantically to scramble toward the remaining glacier surface.

And then, miraculously, a form emerged from behind an ice mount, lit like a golden god from the gleaming sun behind her.

"Hang on, Mariah!"

Patrick! He was clad warmly, too, his face shrouded with a scarf, but that tall, substantial form was definitely his.

In moments, he was at the land's edge of the separating ice.

"Back up, get momentum and ski over here," he shouted. "I'll catch you."

Could she do it?

No choice. At least the crack hadn't yet fully separated where she stood from the rest of the glacier.

She obeyed Patrick. Backed up on her skis. Pushed forward, sailing over the slowly widening void. Her eyes huge, her body shaking. Would she make it this time?

And then, suddenly, she was in Patrick's arms. Held tightly against him. Looking into his beloved brown eyes.

Beloved?

"Thanks," she whispered as the cracking behind her became a roar.

"Let's go!" He grabbed her arm. Together they skied quickly away from the edge.

When they stopped and turned, the ice had again separated, eliminating a substantial part of what remained of Kaley Glacier. Mariah stared toward where she'd been standing—now a void.

The sun had just reached the edge of the horizon and was beginning to settle below it, its glow receding. They would not have light much longer to look down into the water and watch what had happened to the newest ice floe, at least not until the moon had risen.

But Mariah wanted to see all she could. "Come on," she said to Patrick as she eased her way toward the new edge.

He let go of her arm. She didn't look toward him until he said, "You shouldn't have come here, Mariah. And now you're on your own. You'll need to find your way back to town yourself."

Shocked, she turned but he had disappeared. There

were plenty of icy mounds here, of different sizes. He must have ducked behind one.

But why, after helping to save her life—again—had he just left? Right now, she craved the comfort of being with him as she headed back to town.

"Patrick?" she called.

No answer.

Okay. He'd helped her, sure. But why just leave her here? Anger started warring with her shock, terror and relief. She didn't need him…now.

She pulled out her camera from the bag that was over her shoulder. Shot some photos of the ice, including the new, enormous iceberg that surfaced in Tagoga Bay below.

But when she was finished, she still had an urge to look for Patrick.

As she maneuvered around some of the small ice cliffs, she was relieved to see that the edge of the moon had started to appear at the far horizon. In a few minutes, when it rose in the sky, she would be able to see her way back to her vehicle, and civilization, without a light and without Patrick.

But where was he?

She skirted the nearest ice hill, looking for him, and then a few more.

She didn't see him skiing away. Was he hiding from her? But why?

And then she heard something that sounded like a faint moan of pain.

Patrick? Had he been hurt? But why not stay with her, let her help?

She felt disoriented, with all the craggy ice surrounding her, but she nevertheless slid on skis in the direction she thought the sound had come from.

Nothing there, but she heard it yet again and hurried around the next mound. And then another.

She saw him then, kneeling on the ground behind one of the farthest mounds, where the surface was nearly flat beyond it, the full moon now completely visible on the horizon. Patrick was backlighted.

Only—was that Patrick?

As Mariah watched, his tall, fully-clothed form appeared to stand, stretch, then contract as he cried out. The material shrouded him, yet she could see his form writhing beneath it and he shrugged it off—out here, in the cold!

Was he crazy? On drugs?

"Patrick, what's wrong?" she cried, hurrying toward him.

He moaned louder. It sounded more like a growl, an enraged canine's snarl.

As she drew closer, he crouched on the ground on his hands and knees—but he wasn't exactly kneeling. She could see—oh, Lord, what was happening?

His hands and feet receded. Was it a trick of the light? How? His appendages grew smaller, covered in fur. They no longer looked human, but doglike. And when he turned toward her, she could see his features change, agonizingly, from his handsome human face into the visage of a...wolf!

Had *she* unwittingly taken some of his drugs from his mysterious bottle—a hallucinogen? What she was seeing could not be real.

And yet, she recalled, suddenly, what she had read online about the Patrick Worley from Mary Glen, Maryland—home of werewolf legends.

But those stories were unreal. Had to be unreal. She could buy into whatever had gotten him booted out of the military—but not werewolf nonsense. Patrick could not be a shapeshifter. They didn't exist.

Yet the vision in front of her, the form of a silver-gray wolf, pulled its amber-eyed gaze from her and lifted its face toward the full moon.

And howled.

Chapter 11

Mariah hadn't really seen what she thought she had—had she? Quickly, she yanked her camera from her tote bag and started snapping pictures.

The silvery-furred creature growled menacingly, then ran off behind a nearby ice crag.

She attempted to follow, but with all the irregular formations here she could no longer see him. She did, however, hear the diminishing sounds of crunching on the ice that meant something was running away.

"Patrick?" she called. No response.

No surprise.

She returned to the pile of clothing on top of

cross-country skis. They were there. They existed. She couldn't have imagined it all.

When she looked at her photos, the creature on her digital camera was all wolf. No indication that it had been human. *Had* it been human? She could have daydreamed the vision—right?

Patrick could have ditched his belongings. They could have been found by a prowling wolf, and she had seen that creature exploring them.

That was the most logical explanation—except that it meant she had experienced one heck of a hallucination. And Patrick was still out there somewhere, without the clothing she had last seen him in.

No, there was no logic to be found here.

Mariah stumbled as she started skiing slowly back toward her vehicle. She had made her way in daylight. Now, in bright moonlight, she could see well enough, but her body felt as disjointed as if she had fallen apart and sewn herself back together haphazardly.

And her mind? She had yet to put her sanity back on an acceptable track.

So now she knew Patrick's secret. She laughed hysterically into the icy air until she then stopped herself.

What she *knew* was that something had occurred at the edge of Kaley Glacier. Something dangerous that had almost cost her her life.

And when she had been saved—saved herself?— she either hallucinated or had seen something that simply could not happen.

Shapeshifters didn't exist. Her mind was just playing tricks on her, thanks to its recollection of that dumb website that talked about where some Patrick Worley had once lived.

This Patrick Worley had not pulled her to safety, then gone off by himself to change into a werewolf.

Ridiculous…wasn't it?

His rage was vast, yet tinged with sorrow.

He loped forward on the ice, beneath the stunning light of the full moon, barely feeling the frozen arctic air, the bitter chill beneath his paws. Almost unseeing of his surroundings. Ignoring the scents and sounds that were deliciously enhanced while he was in wolf form.

The woman was not supposed to have seen what she did.

But neither was she supposed to have nearly fallen to her death.

A sound penetrated his angry thoughts. A feral growl to his right.

He looked. A grizzly bear raised onto its hind legs, standing its ground along a nearby icy slope, ready to leap into a fight should he draw closer.

But he had other matters to accomplish this night.

He continued on, away from the bear, toward the next glacier.

He slowed down, prowling now. Allowing his anger to recede.

To his left, he heard a grumbling within the ice, near the edge of the closest glacier.

He headed that direction, in time to see the glacier calve.

Not a huge chunk of berg-sized ice, as he had seen so often recently, but a small outcropping of ice from the middle of the glacier.

A calving that, he assumed, was normal.

No explosive sounds. No orca calls. No unusual scents.

No tremendous cracking upheaval that ripped off huge portions of ice and set them adrift.

What made this calving different?

That was what he had been sent here to learn. But at this moment, he only had more questions.

And another difficult situation to deal with—the woman who had seen him shift.

Difficult? No, impossible.

But he had already learned to live with what most humans considered impossible.

Mariah couldn't sleep that night.

Even with the room's temperature turned way up, she lay shivering under the duvet on her bed in the inn. She had left a light on but closed the blind, not wanting to glimpse the full moon and all it reminded her of.

Not that avoiding it helped her forget.

Had she really seen what she'd thought? In any event, what should she do next?

Visit Patrick at the dogsled ranch and ask off-handedly, "Hey, Patrick, did I see you turn into a wolf last night after you saved my life?"

She knew what Harold would want. Her editor would insist that she investigate further. Not just stop at the wildlife photos she had taken last night, including the wolf. He would want her to confront Patrick, get him to admit or deny what she'd seen. Explain it, either way. It wouldn't even have to make a lot of sense. He could then decide which of his publications to include it in—not the one she had signed on to write for, but most likely his gossip rag.

Could she do that?

Dawn. While still in wolf form, Patrick had loped back to where he had changed.

He had not intended his shift to occur in this location during last night's full moon. But neither had he intended, initially, to have to follow Mariah onto the ice and rescue her.

Writhing with sensation and discomfort as always,

he shifted back and stood naked and freezing over his belongings.

Fortunately, everything still seemed to be there. Mariah hadn't run off with his stuff, nor had any glacier creatures. But his clothing was stiff, and covered with ice.

As always, he was prepared—especially now, with no human backup when he shifted. Hoping to act quickly enough to avoid hypothermia, he reached inside his backpack and extracted dry underwear and socks, as well as small, battery-operated heating units. Shivering so hard that it took a lot longer than it should have, he put on his frigid jacket, allowing his minimal body heat to start warming it while he clasped one heating unit to warm his hands and held others against his clothes till he could don his woolen shirt and long pants.

At least it was only November. Cold, yes. But it could have been much worse.

As soon as he was able, he began the trek, on skis, back toward his car. Moving quickly helped also to heat him. His skin tingled as it warmed, but he did not believe he'd suffered any frostbite.

His luck was holding. His vehicle was where he had left it, too. He unlocked it and slid inside, quickly turning on the motor and letting the increasing heat roll over him.

Next time, he would ask his superiors for an Alpha Force assignment in Florida or Hawaii.

Once Patrick's hands had thawed enough to easily control the steering wheel, he called Major Drew Connell.

"How'd everyone do last night?" Patrick asked, driving slowly along the ice-slicked narrow road toward the highway. All shapeshifting members of Alpha Force would have changed last night under the full moon, no matter what animals they shifted into. And no matter where they were.

"No problems," Drew said, then paused. "You sound…were you okay without a handler? Did you shift safely, where you couldn't be seen?"

Patrick's turn to pause. "Not exactly." He described what had happened, why he'd followed Mariah to Kaley Glacier. What he had heard, smelled and seen. And how he'd had to pull her back to safety moments before the sun set and he started his shift.

"She saw you change?" Drew's voice was ominously quiet.

"Yeah," Patrick said tersely. He turned onto the main road toward town. "Couldn't be helped."

"Maybe not. But what will you do about her now, damn it? She writes articles for national publications, about wildlife, right? And now she knows you're among the wildest."

Patrick couldn't help laughing at that, and felt somewhat relieved when he heard Drew chuckle, too.

But it was far from being a laughing matter.

"I haven't had much time yet to figure things out," he told Drew. "But I'll have to talk to her. Reason with her. Explain, without giving up more secrets, why it's a matter of national security that she not say anything." Something occurred to him. "What if I ask if she'd be willing to get a quick security clearance, then become my backup here, assuming she passes? It's a way to keep her from writing about it."

"Bad idea."

"But you did something similar when Melanie learned the truth about you and Alpha Force. Of course she'd suspected it, but—"

"My wife and I were already involved by then," Drew reminded him unnecessarily. Dr. Melanie Harding, now Harding-Connell, had been a veterinarian in Mary Glen, Maryland, and Patrick understood that she had seen Drew shapeshift before they had gotten romantically involved—or too involved at least. He heard his superior officer draw in his breath. "You don't mean—hell, Worley, are you sleeping with that writer?"

Patrick turned onto the road that would soon take him to Great Glaciers Dogsled Ranch. "We didn't exactly sleep," he responded wryly.

Drew was silent for a few long seconds. Was

Patrick about to be reamed? Given orders to return to Ft. Lukman without fulfilling his mission?

That might, in some ways, be best, but he'd never failed at anything before. Didn't intend to now.

"Okay, then," Drew said. "Do you trust her?"

Strangely, despite their disagreements, he believed that she'd keep what she'd seen to herself, if he asked her to—if for no other reason than to keep from being labeled nuts.

But more than that…well, there was something about Mariah that he liked. And not just her body.

"Let me talk to her," he told Drew. "I'll ask for her discretion and get a sense of whether she'll comply."

"Fine. But if she's about to start telling the world what she saw, let me know right away. We'll have to figure out how to deal with her, for the good of Alpha Force. Even if it means discrediting her as a journalist. Ruining her reputation. Whatever."

"Right," Patrick said, keeping his reluctance to himself. He hung up as he turned into the ranch's driveway. And considered the best way to approach Mariah. Fast. For the sake of Alpha Force…and her, too.

If her inclination was to blab what she'd thought she'd seen, he needed to learn that ASAP. At least she'd probably wait long enough to stick it into an article in print, and not throw it out on the internet first.

He hoped.

The dogs weren't loose outside that morning in the yard. As Patrick exited his vehicle in the area between the house and mushers' building, Wes Dawes came up to him. "You okay, Patrick?" His face looked even rounder than usual beneath the hood of his parka, and his hands were thrust into his pockets.

"Sure. Why wouldn't I be?"

"Well, you weren't here last night, were you?"

"No. Had somewhere I needed to be." He didn't intend to give any details.

"No problem, but Mariah called early this morning and asked about your availability to take her out sledding later today."

So she was checking up on him? A good thing or not?

"Unless you have me scheduled for something else, I'll be available. I'll call and let her know."

"Okay. And—" He drew a little closer. "I thought you might be on some official business last night, was all. You know I'm available to help whenever you need me."

"Thanks, Wes." But the fewer people who knew the true nature of Alpha Force, the better. And until Patrick was certain Wes had nothing to do with

Shaun's death, he wasn't going to get him more deeply involved.

As Wes headed for the house, Patrick pulled his backpack out of the passenger seat, then dug inside for his cell phone.

He needed to call Mariah.

But before he scrolled down to her number, captured on his cell, he saw her walking along the driveway toward him.

"Hi, Patrick," she called. "I'm ready for another dogsled ride this morning. That okay?" She reached his side and said softly, "I think we need to talk."

Mariah had thought long and hard about what to say to Patrick the next time she saw him.

"Much as I enjoy our outings together," Patrick responded with a sexy, ironic grin, "we'd be better off talking somewhere besides a dogsled ride. Okay?"

"Sure." She attempted to sound casual. "Any ideas?" Like, someplace private. Except for the dogs, they'd always been alone while out sledding. And she felt certain he wouldn't want anyone listening in.

Neither would she, for that matter. She might sound totally off her rocker when she asked the questions she needed to ask.

At least she'd sound that way to someone who'd never seen what she had.

"Let's take Duke for a walk in the woods," he suggested.

"Fine."

"I'll just run this inside and get him." He motioned to the familiar backpack he had hitched over his shoulder.

Did it have the same stuff in it that she had seen inside it…when? Had it only been yesterday when she'd been here, making love with him—and then getting into that nasty argument?

And then there'd been the events of last night…

Patrick soon came back with Duke on his leash. "The path's over there." He gave a gentle tug on Duke's leash. They all walked briskly in that direction.

Once they reached the area covered by bare-limbed trees, Patrick slowed down to let Duke sniff the ground. He turned toward Mariah. Neither said anything for a moment. And then, Patrick said, "Mariah, out there on the ice—"

At the same time, she began, "I never thought—"

They both stopped. And laughed. And then Mariah said, "Okay, you talk. I know I saw something I can't explain, but you can. Or maybe I can. I'm not sure I ever mentioned it, but I looked you up on the internet when I tried to find out something about Shaun after he was killed. I wasn't sure then that you were the same Patrick Worley as one who captured my interest, but…well, looks like you could be the one who came from Mary Glen, Maryland. The former military guy who came from an area where there are lots of legends about werewolves."

"Yeah, that's me." He grew momentarily silent again. "The military thing—well, maybe we'll talk about that later. And about the shapeshifting…it's not easy to discuss it with anyone who hasn't grown up with my background, but understand, Mariah, that people like me—well, we're a lot better off if no one knows about us. And you—"

"I write articles for a national publication about wolves and other wildlife. I get it. There's a natural conflict between us, isn't there?"

"You could say that."

"I just did." She grinned back when he shot her a dubious smile. "Okay, we'll establish some ground rules. I want to understand what I saw, make sure I'm not nuts." But she *was* nuts, wasn't she? "You won't admit to…anything…I gather, unless I promise to keep it quiet and not write about it. Is that where we are?"

"Absolutely."

A small animal—probably a rat—made some noise in the dead leaves at the side of the path, and Duke lunged in that direction. They stopped talking while Patrick got the dog back under control.

And then Mariah said, "Okay, Patrick. You've got my promise. I want to understand, so I'll keep what you tell me to myself, unless you give me permission to write about it. Okay?" And besides, who'd ever believe her if she tried to tell the world about something so extraordinary that she didn't completely believe it herself, even after seeing it?

"That works." He turned and looked at her. His light brown eyes were intense, questioning, as if he tried to find in her expression whether she could be trusted.

"Great." She really wanted him to trust her. Somehow, she wanted for them to get back to where they'd been yesterday, when they'd made love.

But in between, she'd seen him in an entirely different, amazing situation. They could never simply resume being two ordinary people in lust with one another.

"All right." He proceeded to tell her what she expected to hear. Only, she wouldn't have believed a word if she hadn't seen him change from a gorgeous specimen of sexy male human into a delightful specimen of *Canis lupus*—gray wolf.

He had inherited his shapeshifting gene from his mother, he said. His dad, a veterinarian, had been a regular human being. They had lived in Mary Glen as a cover, thanks to the werewolf legends that locals either believed or didn't, but there weren't actually a lot of shapeshifters who lived there.

"Although—" Patrick said, then stopped and looked down at her again.

"Although what?" she prompted.

"Later," he replied and kept walking.

At her prompting, he talked about how it felt to shift, how he had no choice under a full moon, what it was like to have the glorious, enhanced senses of a canine.

"Then—did the stuff I accidentally saw in your backpack have something to do with your shapeshifting abilities?" She asked as if it was the most natural thing in the world to discuss. As if she had accepted his werewolf nature as real.

Well, it *was* real.

But he ignored her question and continued ahead as Duke pulled on his leash. And that irritated Mariah, even as it stoked her curiosity.

She sped up, putting her gloved hand on his arm. "Patrick?"

He still didn't answer directly. Instead, he said, "Have you ever been checked out for a national security clearance?"

What a non sequitur! Or was it?

"No," she said. "Should I have been?"

"Not necessarily. But for this conversation to reach

its natural conclusion, it would help if you had been, or at least were willing to get one."

Was she? Well, why not? But the real question was…why?

"It's probably fine," she said, "as long as there's a good reason."

"Let's go back to the ranch and I'll make some calls," Patrick said. "Maybe get Wes involved to help out. As long as…have you ever done anything that's made you unlikely to qualify for top secret clearance?"

"Nope," she said. "Unless my profession is a problem. But, Patrick, I really—"

"I'll explain once we have you at least initially checked out. But for now—I'd like to know why you were out on Kaley Glacier last evening."

Okay, he was changing the subject. She could only guess why he was so interested in her having a security clearance. Did he somehow work for the government? That was the only thing that would make sense.

But he had been dishonorably discharged from the military…or had he?

Well, no harm in answering his question. "I was out there to satisfy my curiosity. At lunch yesterday with Flynn Shulster, I overheard Carrie Thaxton talking on her cell phone to someone about expecting some big breakage at Kaley Glacier last night."

Patrick grabbed Mariah's arm. His gaze burned into hers. "Who was she talking to? Do you know?"

"I guessed it was her father. Her husband, Jeremy, was in the restaurant, too, sitting at a table."

"Was there anything else? Anything about what would cause the calving?"

Mariah shook her head. "No, that was all. What's this about, Patrick?"

"I can't discuss it with you now," he said. "But we'll check on that security clearance fast. I think you could be of real help to me, Mariah. Are you willing?"

"I need to know more," she deflected him. And yet the excitement dancing in his eyes made her smile. "But…depending on what it is, I'd love to help you."

"You're—" He didn't finish his sentence. Instead, he bent and gave her one heck of a kiss. Once more his touch heated her, everywhere, despite the chilly air around them. Unlike being caught on disintegrating glaciers, this was becoming a habit she ached to repeat. Over and over.

Duke barked behind them, whether in jealousy or agreement Mariah didn't know. Was the dog aware that his master had a lot in common with him?

Almost involuntarily, she kissed Patrick back. As if in acceptance of who, and what he was.

As if to seal a pact she didn't yet understand.

But she would understand it, somehow.

Soon.

Chapter 12

Having Mariah in his arms, kissing her after what she had learned about him…it amazed Patrick, even as his body responded.

He wanted her. But this was not the time or place. And at the moment, he also needed to determine whether recruiting her was in his best interests. And that of Alpha Force.

He pulled back reluctantly. "I want you to come to my apartment," he said. And laughed at the sexy look she shot him in return. "Well, maybe that, too. But I need to go there alone first, get some information together. Talk to…someone about getting you more involved."

"Involved with what? Your…shapeshifting?"

"Yes. But there's a lot more behind what I'm doing than just changing once a month, under a full moon—which was the norm for centuries for my kind."

The look she shot him seemed full of curiosity. "Then that liquid I found in your backpack really is part of it?"

She was being persistent. And he did owe her an answer. Depending on whether he could legitimately tell her any more. And that he didn't know yet.

He pulled gently on Duke's leash and started back in the direction they'd come from. He held Mariah's gloved hand in his.

"Tell me exactly what Carrie Thaxton said on the phone," he prompted, not entirely to change the subject. But he'd had his own suspicions about Emil Charteris and his grant to study the glacier destruction—especially once he had heard from Flynn Shulster about the rental of that small submersible.

Mariah repeated what she had told him before about the side of Carrie's telephone call that she had overheard. Nothing new. He'd have to do more digging. Or she would…*if*.

When they reached the ranch, most of the sled dogs were out in the yard, playing noisily in the snow. Wes watched them.

"Hey, Wes." Patrick gestured to him, and the chunky former Special Ops guy headed their way. As he reached them, Patrick said, "I've got an assignment for you."

At Wes's questioning glance toward Mariah, Patrick said, "No, I haven't told Mariah anything yet but she suspects I'm not here only as a musher." He smiled at her wary expression. "And, no, Wes doesn't have all the answers, either. He only knows part of the equation."

"You do like to keep secrets, don't you?" Mariah didn't sound especially pleased.

"Doesn't everyone? Anyway, Wes, here's what I want you to do. I'd like to have Mariah join you as my backup. For now, the two of you aren't to discuss, even with each other, what you know or suspect about my employer or assignment. Leave it to me to fill you in individually on a need-to-know basis— although, Wes, you already know part of it." And keeping an eye on Wes's fulfillment of this minimal mission might help Patrick get a better sense of his trustworthiness—and how viable a suspect he really was in Shaun's murder. "I'll give you some contact info," he told Wes, "and I want you to work with Mariah to get her a preliminary security clearance. Help her fill out the form, that's the first step—and I'll want to be there for at least part of your discussion. Then you can submit it and follow up for us." And in the meantime Patrick should get a pretty good sense of whether she'd pass the subsequent vetting.

"Just tell me one thing before we go through all this, Patrick," Mariah said.

"What's that?" He wasn't certain he wanted to hear.

"You weren't really dishonorably discharged from the army, were you?"

"No," he admitted, and was glad she didn't ask any more.

Wes agreed to do as Patrick asked, so Patrick pulled a notebook from his backpack and wrote down the contact data for the head security officer stationed at Ft. Lukman, who would supply the official clearance form.

Patrick relaxed a little as he watched Wes and Mariah enter the main house, glad to have at least a few minutes out of their presence. He followed Duke up the steps of the back building toward his apartment. He intended to strategize further over the phone with Drew and his wife—about what he could, and could not, reveal to Mariah. He wouldn't mention that he had already admitted that his ostensible military history was a lie, part of his cover.

He would also talk to the Alpha Force commanding officer, General Greg Yarrow, bringing him up to speed on what was going on around here, including Mariah's knowledge of his shapeshifting ability. He hoped that would spur the general to do everything possible to push through Mariah's initial security clearance—fast.

And during her initial vetting, as long as there weren't any obvious skeletons in her magazine writer's closet, he would reveal the minimum necessary to get her started in helping him fulfill his mission.

If being with her led to more of that great sex, even better. But that was all. He had no room for any kind of real relationship in his life, now or ever. Despite what Drew Connell shared with his non-shapeshifting wife, Melanie, there were limits on how close Patrick would get to Mariah. His parents had shared a lot, too—really loved each other—and had suffered for it.

Inside his place, Patrick laid his backpack on the kitchenette's floor and put some water into a mug that he thrust into the microwave. Taking out a jar of instant coffee, he waited till the water boiled and made himself a good, strong cup.

And then he pulled out his cell phone and began making calls.

Mariah sat in the Daweses' living room with a cup of coffee brewed by Wes. She figured she'd want the caffeine to assist her through the interrogation to come.

She needed security clearance to get more information from Patrick? And he was still in the military—or at least somehow, most likely, affiliated with the government?

She was definitely intrigued. And miffed that he hadn't told her more yet.

Patrick soon walked into the room with Duke at his heels, followed by Wes. Both men held coffee mugs, too, and Wes also carried a few sheets of paper.

Mariah was glad that the generic beige sofa where she sat was comfortable. She would need all the comfort she could get to handle these men's questions.

Wes sat down on the opposite end of the couch, and Patrick took a seat on a mismatched plaid armchair across the coffee table from them. Duke circled, then lay down at his feet.

There was a large fireplace against the outside wall that needed a good scrubbing to remove soot, and the hardwood floor was scuffed and unpolished. The place definitely looked lived-in, and Mariah found it charming.

But her temporary relaxation while surveying her surroundings ended abruptly when Wes started the inquisition. "Some of this you can just fill out yourself, but in the interest of time I've got to let my contact know anything that's potentially controversial, so we can get your background check started." He began asking things like all her former addresses, everywhere she had gone to school and whether she had ever used a different name.

She recalled nearly all the information he sought, although she stumbled over a zip code or two. She'd been engaged once, but not married, so her name had never changed, but no need to mention the engagement—or what a louse her fiancé had turned out to be once he realized her family's wealth had disappeared.

And then he got into her employment history. "I'd worked in a national park during holidays while I was in college," she said. "I loved it, and really utilized my background of studying for my degree in Natural Resources and Environmental Science." But her parents' finances had started to turn sour while she was still in school, and when she got out she decided to find something that paid better than she could earn as a park ranger.

She wound up working at a Chicago newspaper, and eventually became an investigative reporter. Until the scandal that rocked her family surfaced—her dad, a partner at a large investment firm, had been skimming funds from his clients to make up for his own losses.

And then she wasn't simply a reporter any longer. She was part of the story.

She had been delighted to find the job at *Alaskan Nature Magazine,* where she could live far from the disgrace. Her salary was halved, and she'd had to promise her boss to stay versatile and write for some of the other publications he owned when he asked her to. But for the past three years she had primarily stuck to researching and writing wonderful stories about Alaskan wildlife. And loved it.

"But you were, and are still, an investigative reporter?" Patrick demanded.

"I was. And I could be again, yes. My boss requires me to do some writing for his other publications, and they include a weekly newspaper and a tabloid. But I definitely won't write about anything I understand to be confidential." She stared straight into his expressionless but gorgeously male face. Did he recognize she was telling him wordlessly that she wasn't about to write a story on his shapeshifting—a talent she believed Wes might not know about?

She gave Wes the particulars about her former and current employers and their addresses, which he appeared to write on the forms in his lap. He asked about any problems she might have had with police beyond standard traffic tickets.

She mentioned being questioned by the feds who were after her dad. "But no one ever accused me of anything."

After a few more questions, Patrick rose. "Sounds as if things here are progressing well. I'll check back with you in a little while." And then he left the room.

Leaving Mariah wondering exactly where he was going. Had she said something that bothered him?

Well, of course she had. She'd been an investigative reporter, and she'd been included in a federal investigation. Did that mean he would, ultimately, tell Wes not to bother submitting her info to start her official security clearance?

And would he use that as an excuse to demand that she not reveal to the world those secrets of his that she already knew about—while refusing to tell her anything else?

He'd heard enough.

Of course Patrick had some doubts. But Mariah wasn't an investigative reporter—although she'd been a little cagey about that. She did write for publications besides the nature magazine. And her family had been in trouble.

But she'd moved away from them. And Patrick had little choice about trusting her. She already knew too much about him.

He let Duke sniff around the driveway for a minute till the dog did what was necessary outside, then led him toward the back building.

Patrick waited until he had once more reached the seclusion of his small apartment before calling

Drew again. "Wes Dawes is still with Mariah. He'll finish getting her information, insert it into the form and email it to start her clearance. But there'll be information on it that could cause the general some consternation."

When Patrick had revealed it, Drew said, "Causes me some consternation, too. But do you trust her?"

"With my life," he said—and realized he meant it.

"Well, call the general, tell him what you told me. If he's okay with your jumping the gun and getting her started helping you, that's fine with me."

By the time Wes finished taking down information, Mariah felt exhausted.

And worried. Where had Patrick gone? He hadn't returned. Was he disgusted with what he'd heard?

Well, too bad. She wasn't ashamed of who she was or anything she had done.

She had already promised him that she wouldn't reveal his shapeshifting abilities to anyone. Even if he told her that he wasn't going to work with her, she wouldn't break that promise.

But she would be left with a tremendous void inside her. She wanted to know more about him and all he could do with his shifting.

And despite that so very unexpected side of him, she had come to care for him.

Not to mention crave the sex that she had only been introduced to...

"Okay, I'll go type this up," Wes said. "You'll be able to review and sign it before I send it off, but this way I'll be able to answer any initial questions that arise in the clearance process. Hopefully it'll save us some time."

"Thanks, Wes." She stood. She had wanted to at least be able to say goodbye to Patrick—hopefully not for the last time—before she returned to town. "Please let Patrick know I'll look forward to hearing how this turns out."

"Patrick can tell you right now that it's turning out well," said Patrick from the door to the hall. He entered the living room with Duke again at his feet. "We still need to complete the official process, of course, but I've got the go-ahead to get you started."

Mariah was enthralled. And even a little frightened.

Patrick had driven them to an edge of the glacier field that she had not yet visited.

She had a special reason for being there this night. She was to be Patrick's backup.

He had trusted her enough to tell her that he was part of a covert military unit: Alpha Force. Although he didn't say much about it, she gathered he wasn't the only member who was a shapeshifter. Amazing!

She recalled that Emil Charteris had suggested that what was happening at the glaciers was being caused intentionally by the U.S. government. If so, why send Patrick to learn what was happening?

Unless his mission was to ensure that no one figured out the truth.

But he had trusted her, and for now, at least, she would trust him.

And get as involved as he allowed her to with his astonishing ability to change into a wolf.

The wolf. The one she had seen here before, which had so enthralled her.

Had she recognized Patrick on some level?

He had explained the shifting process as he'd driven. Sounded simple enough. Sort of.

And now they were parked way off the road, yet not far onto the ice.

"During daylight," he said, "while I'm not out mushing, I talk to people around here as much as possible—civilians, cops, tourists—to learn who's seen the calving and when and where. I just act like an interested new resident, make notes later, try to figure out some kind of pattern, though I haven't been successful yet—or learning about who killed Shaun. At night, I go out on the glaciers whenever possible, shifted, so my senses are enhanced, trying to absorb whatever information I can. That's what I'm after tonight. You ready?" The smile he shot her, in the vehicle's faint inside light that he had turned on, made her insides somersault. Damn, but he was one sexy guy—even with the night's incredible activities pending.

Maybe because of them, although Mariah certainly had never considered that something as unbelievable as a gorgeous man changing into a beautiful wolf could be a turn-on.

"Definitely," she responded, realizing she meant it.

Patrick turned and grabbed his backpack from the seat behind them. He pulled out the bottle of liquid that Mariah had found so mysterious only a few days before.

The bottle that had led to such anger and mistrust between them.

It had become a symbol to her of all that Patrick was.

He grabbed a small plastic cup from the pack, unscrewed the top of the bottle and poured some liquid. "Here goes." He drank it, then pulled the light from the pack, too, and opened the vehicle's door.

Outside, on the ice, he turned on the battery-operated lantern. Its light was bright—the intensity,

Mariah knew, of a full moon. The nearby glacial ice shimmered beneath it, giving a surreal glow to the entire, craggy area.

She bit her lip beneath the scarf she had wrapped around her face as she watched Patrick step into the light.

"Keep close watch over me," he said, still smiling. "But no pictures."

"Got it."

He began shedding his clothes despite the cold, although he kept his jacket over his shoulders.

And then the expression on his face changed into one that suggested pain but apparently wasn't. He'd already told her there was discomfort associated with the stretching and bending in his shift, as every part of him changed size and configuration. But it was a discomfort he had long ago grown used to.

Mariah swallowed hard as she saw Patrick's shape distort, even as his face elongated, the slight shadow of his beard lengthening into silvery fur.

"Oh, Patrick," she whispered, unsure whether to be enchanted by what she saw or sorrowful. They were very different, and yet he was so magnificent as, soon, he shook off the remaining clothing he had worn as a man and leaped away from them, a gorgeous wolf.

He looked at her, his eyes clearly cognizant of her and who she was. *Really* amazing!

"Let's go explore the glacier, Patrick," she said. "I've got your back."

Hours later Patrick once again sat behind the steering wheel of his car. Mariah was in the passenger seat. They were nearly ready to head back to the dogsled ranch, where Mariah would stay the rest of the night with Patrick in his small apartment.

"No calving at all tonight," he confirmed. "I didn't see any, even when I went off on my own."

"Any sounds that weren't normal?" she asked. She amazed him. Somehow she seemed to have accepted this night's occurrences as if they happened every day.

Which they could, for him. But for her…

"Nothing this time." He reached across the console and placed his hand behind her neck, drawing her closer.

She seemed to hesitate for a second, staring inquisitively into his face.

"You okay with everything?" he asked, suddenly uncertain, and not happy about it. What if she found being his backup acceptable—but not *him?*

Her smile was radiant—and sexy as hell—as she said, "Much to my amazement, I'm more than okay with everything, Patrick." And then she leaned toward him and gave him one hot, suggestive kiss—a harbinger of what he eagerly anticipated for the rest of this night.

Chapter 13

The next day, Mariah was exhausted. And exhilarated.

Sure, she had always adored animals, especially wildlife. But who would have imagined that someone like Patrick even existed—or was so intriguing while in wolf form?

Even better, he was incredibly sexy—a guy who was imaginative and sublimely energetic in bed.

She was back at the B and B now. Speaking of bed, the one in her room looked appealing. After being with Patrick during his changes the night before, she had joined him in his apartment at the dogsled ranch—where they'd been in bed, sure. But she had gotten virtually no sleep.

She had notes to enter onto her computer now, for her article. She couldn't allow the opportunity to slip by to describe the wildlife she had seen last night, on the ice.

The *real* wildlife. She would definitely keep her promise to Patrick and not mention the wolf who had so enthralled her last night. But there were other wolves that were appropriate for her to write about. She'd seen three of them who had apparently been attracted to a potential new pack member, and had stalked toward Patrick at one point.

She had snapped their pictures, but none of the part-time canine they had come to visit.

She had also seen a pair of grizzly bears, visible in the distance beneath the now-waning moon.

Who knew what other wildlife wonders she might see tonight on the ice? Since, during daylight in human form, Patrick had experienced nothing vital in his quest to understand the decline of Great Glaciers National Park, he was going to change again, and she would once more be his backup.

Incredible, how much she loved the idea!

And might even love him…

Her cell phone rang, and she pulled it from her bag. It was Patrick.

"Hi," she said, amused at her own breathlessness.

"Hi. You doing okay?"

"Sure am. You?"

"I'm looking forward to tonight."

"Me, too." She laughed. "We sound like a couple of shy kids who don't know what to say to each other."

"Yeah. But like I said—"

"I can't wait until tonight," she finished.

They fell into a pattern over the next week. Mariah would take catnaps in the afternoon, then either show up at the dogsled ranch in the evening or meet Patrick at Fiske's for a quick dinner first.

And to help him, she, too, asked questions not only about wildlife but about who had seen glaciers calving and the circumstances surrounding the events. She'd passed on to Patrick the few snippets of information she'd gathered.

Later, they would take her SUV and go out in the field, usually onto the glaciers. There, Patrick would change and prowl the area. Mariah would watch as he shifted, then follow to ensure his safety.

She also got really great pictures of some of the area's nocturnal animals, usually because the weather was clear and the waning moon provided enough light. Occasionally, she would bring Patrick's magic light with her and set it up to help in her photography. She located more grizzly bears, some bats, flying squirrels and even lizards, as well as sea otters and sea lions in the bay.

And had a marvelous time with her research.

Several times, they were out on the ice when another horrendous calving occurred, although not, fortunately, nearby. The wolf that was Patrick would always lope off in that direction, but he told Mariah, once he had changed back, that he still hadn't learned the cause.

Most often, their time outside was uneventful.

Out of curiosity, they headed once toward the area where Emil Charteris and his family had established their camp—found thanks to a hint from Flynn Shulster, who had previously sailed by it. It was located at a site containing remote tourist cabins, way out of town along the bay.

Mariah didn't get especially close to the camp, though she did see the area from a distance, including the pontoon craft along the dock on which the small submersible was mounted. She assumed everyone was asleep, so it seemed safe enough when Patrick prowled nearby in wolf form.

But he found nothing useful there either, he told her later. No overt indication of how Emil was studying the glaciers. That remained a mystery to Patrick, which utterly frustrated him. Surely, if anyone had an inkling about what caused the glaciers to fall apart so rapidly, it would be the glaciologist who'd been studying them for so many weeks.

Patrick remained determined to find answers, with or without input from Emil Charteris, although he told Mariah that his commanding officer had started talking about a time for him to end his quest and return to his base.

Not something Patrick was pleased about. Especially since he'd hit a dead end as to who had killed his friend—and his official military backup—Shaun.

Patrick kept Mariah apprised about how her security clearance was going, but since only a week had passed nothing was certain.

He had obviously decided to trust her anyway, since he talked freely about his military unit, Alpha Force, and how its shapeshifters and the non-shapeshifting backup members, like her, worked together.

That was sometimes what they would talk about long into the night, back in Patrick's apartment after engaging in extended and delightful bouts of lovemaking. Other times, she would tell him how her article was progressing, and how she continuously parried her boss, friend and editor Harold's inquiries and demands that she spend more time doing investigative journalism—like learning more about the official inquiry into Shaun's murder.

She did ask questions of the appropriate cops now

and then, including Detective Gray and the talkative officer, Pilke. She reported to both Harold and Patrick that, if they were zeroing in on any suspects, they weren't about to tell her.

One thing she didn't tell Patrick, though, was how much she argued with Harold about her assignment here. He wanted her to come back to Juneau with whatever photos and information she already had, and get her damned article written.

She kept putting him off, wanting to remain in town as long as possible. Hinting she might be able to write a story on the murder if she hung out here a little longer—giving no particulars, because she had none.

And, as with Patrick's ongoing discussions about his own mission, she knew their idyllic interlude couldn't last forever.

They had been enjoying their routine for over a week now. Tonight, they would meet for an early dinner at Fiske's. They'd dropped in there often, and Mariah relished their pending obscure discussion of where to head later that night, when Patrick would again change and scour the glacier field for clues about its destiny. It was fun to come up with ways to couch Patrick's quest, and how he would engage in it that night, in vague references that no eavesdropper would be able to interpret.

As always, when she arrived, the place was filled, and the roar of conversations filled the air. No piano, though. The musician must be on a break.

Mariah looked around. No Patrick...not yet. She didn't see anyone else she knew, either—not Emil Charteris or his family, or Flynn Shulster and his entourage of fans.

Spotting a couple rise at the center of the room, she hurried toward their table to stake a claim, crunching her way on peanut shells. She sat on a chair facing the door to watch for Patrick.

"Glass of wine?" Thea Fiske asked, her pen poised, as always, over the pad of paper in her hand. "Beer?"

"Wine, please," Mariah said. "The house red."

"Waiting for someone?" Thea's wide grin was suggestive. Mariah knew the bar owner had noticed her with Patrick.

"Could be." Mariah smiled back—just as the loud conversations around her suddenly hushed.

Confused, she met Thea's scowl. Then the woman stared toward the door. Mariah glanced that way and saw Patrick. He met her gaze and started toward her.

"Another one of those omens." Thea shook her head so vehemently that her plait of gray hair seemed to vibrate.

"But that superstition—"

"Last time it happened that musher was murdered, right?"

Mariah couldn't argue with that.

"Killer's still out there," Thea said. "Mark my words, something else'll happen. Be careful." Thea waddled off, her short, squat form disappearing into the noisy crowd.

"Are you okay?" Patrick pulled the other chair out and sat, looking quizzically at Mariah. The room again buzzed with conversations. The omen—or silly coincidence—was over.

"I'm fine." Mariah aimed a sexy smile toward him. "And looking forward to our evening." She felt her expression fade. "But did you notice the way the place got so quiet? I'm not superstitious, but—well, I've learned there are things in this world that people generally don't believe in." This time her smile was brief and wry. She described the silence the first time she had noticed him walk into Thea's, and what the restaurateur had said about it. "She claimed this evening that it had been a harbinger of Shaun's murder—and it just happened again."

"Interesting, but we've got other things to worry about."

"Like?"

"Like what to order for dinner. And our plans for later this evening."

He obviously wasn't worried. And if anyone

believed in woo-woo kinds of stuff, surely Patrick would be among them. Mariah began to relax.

But she was glad to sip her red wine when Thea brought it over. It might take some of the edge off her concerns.

Patrick and she both ordered pot roast and potatoes, the day's special. Thea served it fairly quickly, with a meaningful glance that Mariah interpreted to be an ongoing warning.

She appreciated the woman's concern, she supposed, but there were more things to worry about than superstitions.

Like, would Patrick find any new clues about the glacier issues while prowling tonight, or anytime soon? Would she be able to help him learn anything new?

And would she see, and be able to photograph, any as-yet-unseen form of local wildlife for her article?

They soon finished eating, and Patrick paid their tab despite Mariah's offer to split it. They walked out of the restaurant together, and Mariah immediately noticed both the chill and the silence as the door closed behind them.

But Mariah didn't have time to get cold before he bent down and set her on fire with a kiss that suggested all they would do much later tonight. "You ready?" he asked.

"Always."

They were only partway down the block, heading toward Patrick's car this time, when Mariah heard running footsteps behind them. Patrick turned as she did.

Carrie Thaxton seemed frantic as she caught up with them. "I'm so glad I found you, Mariah. My father—I can't believe what he's doing with those poor animals. Jeremy is with him, trying to talk him out of it, but I never thought my own father..."

"What animals?" Mariah asked. "And what's he doing?"

"Wolves. He's killing them, or at least threatening to. I don't understand why, but he says it's part of his study about what's going on with the glaciers. I think he must be going crazy, though, since he really hasn't given me any answers. I can't call the cops—they might arrest him. But maybe he'll listen to someone else. I hate to ask, but could you come to our camp and help Jeremy and me?"

Patrick got in his car to follow Carrie. He wished he had been able to convince Mariah to stay in Tagoga. Something didn't feel right. But she had insisted on coming along.

He would simply have to protect her. Only, it might not be so simple. In any event, his handy backpack was behind his seat. As usual, when he was outside his apartment, it held more contents than those he needed for shifting.

As he drove, he made a couple of calls. Unable to reach Wes Dawes, he left a message. "Mariah and I are on our way to the research camp maintained by Emil Charteris and his family. His daughter, Carrie, asked for our help. Do me a favor, and put the local cops on notice that there might be something going on. Hopefully, I'll be able to use this visit for some research, too. I'll call again if we need assistance."

His next call was to his commanding officer. But since Major Drew Connell was thousands of miles away, at Ft. Lukman in Maryland, all he could do was report where he was going and why.

"Just so you know, I've got someone on his way to act as your backup," Drew told him. "Should arrive in a few hours. Can you wait till then?"

"No way." But he did give Drew what information he could about the location of Emil Charteris's camp. "In case he gets here and can't reach me immediately on my cell phone, tell him to head there."

"Roger that," Drew told him. "And…be careful, Patrick."

"I'll be fine. Mariah's got my back." He smiled at her, even as the silence at the other end of the phone shouted Drew's dubiousness about how effective Mariah might be. Or even whether she could be trusted. "I'll report in later," he finished, and hung up.

Carrie led them along icy back roads outside Tagoga. The route was different from the one they'd taken a couple of nights earlier when they had peeked at Emil Charteris's base camp.

"What do you really think is going on, Patrick?" Mariah asked as he slowed on an icy curve.

"Don't know," Patrick said. "But we need to stay alert. And you need to remember that I'm the one with military training. Promise you'll listen to me."

"And obey your orders?" Her tone sounded half amused and half irritated.

"Yeah," he said. "Obey my orders."

He knew better than to think she would do so without question. She wasn't in the military.

He would have to give her good reasons for whatever he might command her to do.

And only hope she complied.

They eventually reached the camp. Patrick parked beside Carrie's SUV. Mariah was gratified when he hurried around to help her out on the slick surface, and smiled when he hefted his backpack from the rear seat.

It was still a short while until sunset, so it was easy to make out the cabins and dock with the pontoon boat that held the small submersible.

The place looked the same as the last time they'd been by. But Mariah changed her mind as they started up the paved walkway toward the cabins. Blood spattered the ice at the side of the cleared path. Even worse, there were chunks of bloody muscle from some poor animal.

Mariah gasped. "Oh, no." She'd thought Carrie was exaggerating what her father was up to, yet this was evidence of the slaughter of animals. But why?

"Come on." Carrie hurried ahead of them. Mariah hadn't paid attention before, but the boots, warm slacks, jacket and snug hat worn by Emil's daughter all appeared dressier than called for at a scientific campsite. Had she returned from somewhere else and seen what her father had done?

"Wait here," Carrie whispered at the door to the largest wooden cabin. "I'll go in and see what's happening now."

Mariah exchanged glances with Patrick. This seemed so odd. Yet, they'd seen the horrible evidence of animal cruelty and worse.

"Fine," he said. "Let us know what we can do." Once Carrie had disappeared into the house and shut the door behind her, he held out his key and said, "Now's the time for you to get back into the car and call Wes. Tell him to send the cops."

"What you can do now," came a female voice from the side of the building as Carrie reappeared, pointing a gun at them, "is to go inside for a little talk. Don't even think about it," she said to Patrick, who had thrust his hand into his backpack. "I assume you have a gun, so let me have that." She got closer and yanked Patrick's backpack away. "Now open the door and go in."

Mariah again looked at Patrick. He gave her a reassuring look that she hoped was more than just an attempt to comfort her.

With luck, he had a plan.

But her hopes were chilled when they walked onto the cabin's wood floor. Emil Charteris wasn't there, and neither were any animal remains.

Instead, Carrie's husband, Jeremy, was slumped on a chair in the middle of the room. He looked unconscious. And bloody.

And even though Mariah still had no idea what was going on, she had a sinking feeling that Carrie intended that Patrick and she share Jeremy's fate. She rushed over and knelt to check the man. He had a pulse, but he didn't wake up, even when she touched him.

"What's going on, Carrie?" Patrick demanded. "Why bring us here to see what you did to your husband?"

"You're jumping to conclusions," Carrie huffed. "I told you my father is acting nuts. What makes you think I'm the one who harmed Jeremy?"

"Your gun, for one thing," Mariah said quietly, rising. She recalled the silence at Fiske's earlier that night and Thea Fiske's superstition that it meant death. Shaun's murder had supported that possibility.

Was Jeremy Thaxton dying? Or, might the superstition come true because of her death, or Patrick's?

"Well, I couldn't take the chance on your running away. Not when I have to find out… Tell me what you were doing here the other night, Mariah. I saw you snooping around."

The night she had come to this area with Patrick while, in shifted form, he looked around? No way would she mention that.

"You know I'm researching local wildlife," Mariah responded. "I've been exploring different parts of the glaciers and surrounding areas, taking pictures of anything I might use in my article. I was here that night just seeing what I could see. If I'd seen you, I'd have come over to say hi. Maybe ask about your wildlife statistics. You'd said once you would share them, even though Jeremy and your father weren't as accommodating."

"I lied." Carrie's grin looked snide.

"What are you really doing here, Carrie?" Mariah asked.

"None of your business, which is entirely the point." Approaching Mariah, she brandished her gun.

"You're not what you claim to be, are you, Mariah? I looked you up online and found a bunch of articles you wrote a while back that required prying into things that didn't concern you. You were getting a fair reputation as an investigative journalist, in fact—at least until your family became the subject of those kinds of stories. You lay low for a while and wrote cutesy articles on wildlife for your Alaskan magazine. But you've been much too pushy for me to believe that's all you're doing now. Are you writing an article about us?"

"Only about wildlife," Mariah insisted. "I was especially hoping to get something helpful from Jeremy." She exchanged a brief glance with Patrick. Carrie had turned enough for her confrontation with Mariah that her back was mostly to him, and he was edging toward her. If Mariah could continue to distract the woman… "But your dad—what's happening with him? We saw the evidence of his—someone's—dismemberment of animals on the roads near here. Did Emil do that?"

Carrie laughed. "Of course not. I did it to be sure you'd follow me all the way to check it out. It's stuff I bought at the supermarket, not any of your beloved wildlife." She abruptly stepped sideways and waved the gun between Mariah and Patrick. "Don't think I wasn't aware that you were getting ready to jump me, Mr. Worley. Or should I say, Lieutenant Worley?

You're with the military, aren't you? That's what Wes Dawes told me when I got him drunk enough at Fiske's."

Not a good thing. Patrick had told Mariah he'd had reservations about using Wes as a backup, but more because he couldn't be certain that the musher hadn't been Shaun's killer. His big mouth hadn't been an issue then. But Patrick was supposed to be here undercover.

"My dad got really suspicious of you when I told him what I'd learned," Carrie said. "He's genuinely concerned about what's causing the glacier destruction in Alaska and believes it's the result of government testing in this area. Finding out about a hidden military presence helped to get him really jazzed about his theory."

Mariah turned toward Patrick. Was it possible that he was hiding his real reason for being here from her, even now?

But what would a shapeshifter do to assist the military in any covert project that destroyed the glaciers?

Observe what was going on and people's reactions?

"That's a bunch of crap, Carrie," Patrick said, "and you know it—even if your father doesn't. Were you just encouraging him to go off on this tangent to hide the truth?"

Carrie didn't respond. That intrigued Mariah. Did it mean Patrick was right?

That suggested Carrie knew the truth. And that it had nothing to do with the government.

"You're just guessing." Carrie sounded almost bored, but it didn't mean she had relaxed her guard.

"How did your dad know about the calving on Kaley Glacier?" Mariah asked.

"What do you mean?" Carrie looked confused.

"I heard you talking on the phone with him the other day, when I was at Elegance Restaurant for lunch. I heard you say something about major breakage."

Carrie laughed. "Oh, I wasn't talking to…never mind. Get over there, both of you." She waved her gun toward a battered sofa leaning against the far wall. "Go sit down."

"No, really," Patrick pressed as he took Mariah's arm and led her toward the couch. "What's going on with the glaciers? I'll bet you know. Is your father involved and only pretending to be studying the glaciers to figure it out?"

"You're way off base," Carrie said with a laugh.

"What's the truth, then?" Patrick cajoled. "You obviously intend to kill us, and we wouldn't be able to tell anyone else."

Was he nuts? Mariah hadn't assumed they were

going to die…or had she? That superstition. Maybe it would come true yet again.

"I'm not telling you anything." The sound of a car's engine sounded faintly from outside. Carrie smiled. "But that doesn't mean you won't learn something before you die. I don't think you need to hear, but maybe he'll tell you anyway. Add to the fun, since you won't be able to do a damned thing about it. In any case, it's showtime."

Chapter 14

In a minute, Emil Charteris walked into the cabin. He looked around. Not having much choice, Mariah remained on the couch beside Patrick, watching Emil warily. Waiting for him to take charge of the situation. He always appeared in control of the others in his family. Had he set this up? Why?

"What's going on here, Carrie?" he asked. "I thought we'd agreed to wait before we handled these people. And—Jeremy! What the hell happened to him?"

Carrie edged quickly toward her father, still holding the gun on Mariah and Patrick. "He'll be okay, Dad. But he started asking too many questions.

And I also needed something to distract these two when I got them here."

"Yeah, we were definitely distracted," Patrick said. Mariah shot him a warning glance. She didn't think that antagonizing anyone was a good idea at the moment—not till they had a better grasp of what was going on. He had shifted away from her but remained on the couch. His eyes stayed on Carrie, but he glanced briefly, now and then, toward his backpack, which Carrie had dropped on the floor near the door. Did he have a weapon in there, as Carrie had suggested?

She knew what else he had in his bag, but using it now seemed out of the question—even if it could be of help.

Emil's long, craggy face sagged, and his eyes grew rheumy. "I don't understand how they're involved in all this, Carrie." His voice was a sad whine, as if he had suddenly withdrawn into childhood. He certainly didn't seem in charge at this moment. That raised a slew of additional questions. "Andy, do you get it?" He turned back toward the door he had just entered. The piano player from Fiske's stood there, hunched over and blinking behind his thick glasses. His pallor was emphasized by his white jacket. Why was he here? He hadn't seemed particularly friendly with Emil at the bar/restaurant.

"No, sorry, Emil, I don't. But maybe we can figure this out."

"Okay." Emil straightened to his full height, as if taking control once more. "Let's start with an explanation, Carrie. Did these people tell you why they hurt Jeremy? What are they even doing here?" He rounded on Mariah. "I thought you wanted information on local wildlife from Jeremy, Ms. Garver. He wasn't permitted to give interviews, just like I couldn't. But that's no reason to hurt him this way."

Emil was clearly confused, his mental state unstable. He already knew what had happened to Jeremy. "I'm not the one who hurt him, Emil," Mariah began, but Carrie approached, raising the gun as if intending to strike Mariah with it.

"Don't try to make excuses, Mariah. We all know that you're getting desperate for information for your damned article, and that you'd go to any lengths to get what you need."

"I'm doing fine with my research," she retorted, "no thanks to you and your family. And I certainly wouldn't stoop to hurting anyone to get another quote or two." She turned toward Emil. "Your daughter admitted doing this to her husband, Emil. What we don't understand is why."

Patrick had stayed awfully quiet. Mariah assumed he was planning an escape, or some other way to save them. How could she help? She aimed another glance in his direction. His expression was stony, unreadable. He had moved even farther to the end of the sofa. Was he thinking of doing something—like rushing Carrie and her gun?

"I did it for fun." Carrie's laughter sounded so carefree that Mariah couldn't help staring. Was the woman insane? That was one possible explanation for what she had done to her husband—and why she had brought them here under pretense. But Mariah didn't buy it.

"Don't be ridiculous," Emil told his daughter. "Now let's take care of Jeremy. Does he need to go to a hospital?"

"I don't think so, Mr. Charteris," Andy Lemon piped in. "Doctors would ask too many questions, and we don't want to get Carrie into trouble." He now stood directly behind Carrie, bent as if in front of a piano keyboard.

"If you want to keep Carrie out of trouble, Andy," Patrick said, "I'd suggest you get that gun away from her before she hurts anyone else."

"Oh, but then she might hurt me," the piano player said in a small, meek voice. He laughed suddenly and stood up straighter, no longer in his characteristic slouch. He peeled off his glasses and shoved them into his pocket. "But that ain't gonna happen, is it, honey?"

He put his arms gently around Carrie, who raised her mouth for a kiss—but without moving the gun she still had pointed in the general direction of the couch where Mariah and Patrick sat.

"No, you SOB!" Jeremy Thaxton's voice was surprisingly strong, considering his injuries and the fact he'd just emerged from unconsciousness. Mariah hadn't been paying attention to him, and apparently no one else had, either. He sprang from his chair and ran toward Andy Lemon, who still had an arm around Carrie. "Leave my wife alone!"

"Oh, I don't think she'll be your wife much longer," Andy said calmly, sidestepping so Jeremy stumbled as he reached for him. Andy gently took the gun from Carrie and aimed it toward Jeremy's head. "Now go back and sit down like a good boy, or I'll have a wonderful time making her a widow instead of a soon-to-be divorcée."

When Jeremy didn't move, Andy struck him in the neck with the butt of the gun. Jeremy crumbled to the floor—but the action had apparently been enough of a diversion for Patrick to act. He launched himself toward Andy, too—and there was nothing hesitant in his movement. He looked all efficient, all military, easily able to bring down an opponent in hand-to-hand combat. He grabbed Andy Lemon's gun hand while knocking him to the floor.

"No, you son of a—" Lemon shouted.

"Get away from him!" Carrie shrieked and leaped onto Patrick's back, knocking him off balance. Mariah ran toward the melee, unsure what she could do to help.

The gun discharged. A bullet whizzed by Mariah's ear, and she screamed.

"Stay back," Patrick yelled. He was still struggling with the others. Neither had his combat background, but the sheer force of two against one kept the odds against Patrick. No way would Mariah stay away.

Carefully yet quickly, she moved behind them. How could she get control of that damned gun? It was the key to ending this.

"Stay back, Mariah," Emil Charteris said. She had almost forgotten his presence in the turmoil. "You could get hurt."

"But we have to stop—"

"Oh, we'll do that." Only then did Mariah realize he had an ulu in his hand—and it was poised near her throat. She'd seen similar native Alaskan knives being sold to tourists, each a deadly looking curved blade on a wooden handle. She'd considered them interesting souvenirs.

This one was a threat.

"Oh, Patrick, see this?" Emil called. "Now, give up that gun and leave my daughter alone."

Mariah wanted to struggle. To tell Patrick she was fine, to do what he needed to.

But to say anything at all could end her life.

Patrick's gaze had flown upward. For an instant, his studied blankness morphed to horror and dismay.

"Leave her alone, Emil," he growled.

"You know my terms."

Patrick's eyes met Mariah's.

Slowly, he released Andy's hand and put both of his in the air.

Damn.

If Mariah wasn't here, if Patrick didn't have to watch out for her, things would be different. He'd subdue these criminals, forcing them to reveal all he needed to know before getting local authorities involved.

And if he couldn't do it by using his regular military training, he'd find a way to grab his bag and take full advantage of his own special skills. In fact, that was exactly how he wanted to handle this. And not by using just the 9 mm semiautomatic pistol he had hidden in there.

But without the time to get it, it wouldn't be easy. And he knew the risks of trying to take control—and failing.

Especially since Mariah *was* here. He'd risk his own life, but not hers. So, for now, he had to play along. When Emil told him to go back and sit on the sofa, he did.

And accepted Mariah's angry glare with equanimity. "You shouldn't have backed down," she hissed so low that no one else was likely to have heard. "Don't worry about me."

"Your neck's too pretty for me to have done anything else." He watched her frown melt, if just a little.

And wished he could grab her and hold her close. Soothe her. And calm his own ragged nerves until he could act.

So here they were. In mortal danger. Unsure of allies and enemies, although Jeremy might be among the former. Patrick glanced where he lay on the floor. Jeremy remained unconscious again, but rhythmic movement of his chest showed that he was still alive.

And Andy Lemon? He was the real unknown in the mix. What was he even doing here? Did Carrie and he have something going on? That's what their prior embrace implied. Jeremy had apparently taken it that way, too.

So—could he distract these three by setting them against one another? Unlikely, as between father and daughter. And daughter and possible lover Lemon.

Emil Charteris against Andy Lemon? Maybe. Emil wielded a mean ulu. But he wasn't waving it around now. Instead, he'd retreated into the kitchen area and stood by the sink.

Patrick wished he knew more about the rest of this cabin. There was a closed door to their right. It must lead at least to a bathroom. A bedroom, too? Most likely, since there was no bed in here.

His backpack remained near the door where they'd come in.

He ached to get this group under his control by unleashing his wildest self, but that might be impossible.

Still, he'd test things.

"So being a piano playing in Nowhere, Alaska, acts like a chick magnet, Andy?" he asked casually. "I used to plunk out a few tunes on the keyboard. Maybe I should try it. Especially when being a loser in hand-to-hand combat doesn't matter."

"Shut up." Andy had pulled a battered chair from beneath a small table near the kitchen and planted himself in it, massaging his wrist. He was leaving it to Carrie and Emil, using their smaller handgun to control their captives, including Jeremy.

"Well, with all those women after you at Fiske's, and I see now that married lady Carrie's among them—I'm impressed."

"I said—" Andy began, scraping his chair against the floor as he stood.

"I know what you're trying to do, Patrick," Carrie

said, "and it won't work. You don't know anything about how things are between… Andy and me. Or about what Jeremy thinks about it. Or anything else. So just keep your mouth shut."

Patrick caught Mariah's gaze. She, too, seemed to tell him to stay quiet. He shot her a brief, grim smile that she didn't mirror.

"You're right," he said to Carrie. "But I assume Andy's just a fling to you." Interesting, that she had hesitated on Andy's name. Why? "That's obviously all you are to him, judging by the way ladies are all over him at Fiske's when you're not around. I'm jealous. I want lessons."

"You're making a lot of noise for a man whose life's in danger," Emil said. "Why don't you just keep your mouth closed?"

"And here I assumed you'd want your daughter to know the truth about her lover."

Emil waved the ulu. "He's not her—"

"Keep quiet!" Andy shouted, propelling himself from the chair toward them. His fist connected with Patrick's jaw.

Fortunately, the guy's punch was as wimpy as his appearance so it didn't hurt much, but Patrick used the opportunity to grab the guy, turn him and twist an arm around his throat.

But Carrie pressed the pistol to the side of Mariah's

skull. "Let him go, you bastard," she hissed, "or I'll shoot her."

Damn. If she'd threatened Patrick that way, it wouldn't matter much. Oh, yeah, there'd be some pain, but he could only be killed by silver bullets and he doubted that was the composition of their ammo. But she had threatened Mariah instead.

Patrick released Andy, stepped back. The piano player knelt on the floor, holding his neck and choking.

"Austin, darling, are you all right?" Carrie whispered, kneeling beside him without directing the firearm away from Patrick.

"Fine," the guy gasped. "Now, shoot him."

She seemed to consider this, and glared at Patrick. He held up his hands in surrender, half hoping she'd try. He could pretend to be mortally wounded, then catch them off guard. But if she shot him, she might also shoot Mariah.

He still needed to take control of the situation. And to achieve that, he might need to act like a regular human being.

He tried to put on a scared, submissive look. Carrie seemed a bit crazed—crazed enough to kill what she assumed was a normal unarmed man in cold blood?

Apparently not. Patrick felt a modicum of relief as she said, "I can't just kill him that way, but we'll take care of him later. Out on the ice, like we talked about."

"You're too soft," Andy yelled, then started coughing again.

Patrick took the opportunity to sit back on the couch beside Mariah, to demonstrate his compliance—however unwilling.

And as Carrie bent over the choking piano player again, the gun wavering in a way that made Patrick damned nervous about Mariah's safety, he realized what he'd just heard.

Carrie had called the punk on the ground "Austin."

He had heard that name recently.

And suddenly everything that had been happening around Great Glaciers National Park seemed to make sense. His nonscientific investigation might be about to succeed even better than Alpha Force had initially anticipated. Assuming he could end this standoff.

How the hell could he do that?

Well, one step at a time. He needed to confirm his suspicions first.

Mariah stiffened as Patrick whispered into her ear. "I'm going to buy us a little time. And things are about to get interesting."

What was he talking about? How could he—

"So, Austin," he said, "why don't you explain why

you've been blowing up some of your own mines down in the lower forty-eight? I'm really curious."

Austin? Mines? Mariah knew Patrick hadn't been frightened into madness, but this sounded awfully strange.

Andy Lemon was again seated at the scarred table across the room. But as he stopped coughing and glared at Patrick, he was definitely no longer the pale, meek piano player Mariah had seen so often at Fiske's. His shoulders pulled back, his jaw jutted and his formerly pale complexion turned almost florid.

"Who the hell are you talking to, dog-man?"

Mariah blinked. Could he possibly know what Patrick really was?

"I'm talking to you, Austin DeLisio," Patrick replied. "And you know I work at the dogsled ranch? I didn't think someone as exalted as you would even take notice of someone lowly like me. I'm flattered. But you've been spending a lot of time around here lately under an alias and playing the piano, despite all the chaos going on at your mines. Does that mean you're aiming your sights in a different direction?"

Andy—Austin?—stood and swaggered toward Patrick, who didn't move. Andy now had the pistol, which he had taken from Carrie, and he wagged it back and forth as he approached.

Mariah wished she could get to her purse, which Carrie had taken. She wanted her cell phone, to call for help. Plus, she'd love to secretly take pictures of what was going on, and a digital recording. Harold would love that.

And if nothing else, it could be evidence of what had happened here, if Patrick and she weren't around to tell anyone.

But that was not likely to happen.

"I want to know who you really are, Worley," Austin said, confronting Patrick.

"You've got me pegged. I'm Patrick Worley, musher. And how'm I doing about nailing you? You're Austin DeLisio, owner of a bunch of mines and head of an association of major mine owners. But why are you hiding out here—so it won't look like you're involved with the chaos your peons are causing in the mines in the lower forty-eight? And what are you doing that makes the glaciers fall apart?"

"You think you're so smart?" Whoever he was, the man sneered. "I've had you checked out. You're nobody, dumped from the military with a dishonorable discharge and barely able to make a living here as a…or is all of this just a cover?" His last words came out as if he'd suddenly experienced a revelation. "That's it, isn't it? You're still associated with the military or some damned government group, and you're here to find out about the glaciers." The man pointed the gun right at Patrick's face. "And I made it easy for you, didn't I, damn it?"

"Easy? I don't think so. It's taken me longer than I'd hoped to figure out this much. And tell me one more thing—why did you kill my buddy Shaun Bethune?"

Austin's fury was almost tangible. Mariah was certain now that Patrick had identified the man correctly, although she still didn't understand a lot of their exchange. His gun hand trembled as if it was a separate entity from the rest of him, unsure whether to shoot or strike Patrick where he was most vulnerable.

"You want details, you government SOB? I'll give you details."

"What the hell is he talking about?" Emil yelled at the same time, dashing from the kitchen area.

"Nothing, Dad. Stay out of this." Carrie grabbed her father by the arm and attempted to pull him to the other side of the room, but Emil wouldn't budge. "Austin, please keep calm. And quiet. You don't need to tell them anything."

"Oh, but I want to." His grin was suddenly huge and evil, not at all the nerdy little smile of the bespectacled guy playing the piano. "First thing, you're right. I took care of your buddy Shaun since he was not only too nosy, but he was too smart. He was asking a lot of pointed questions around the bar. Sounded like he was already starting to equate the mousy, invisible little piano player with who I really am. Had to take his computer, too, just in case the information was stored there."

Mariah felt Patrick's muscles clench beside her, and she grabbed his arm, keeping him from doing anything foolish—like rushing the man with the gun.

"But I figured you out anyway, so you killed him for nothing, you bastard." Patrick's voice was low and menacing, and wordlessly promised retaliation.

"Could be." Austin didn't sound particularly concerned. "At least no one saw me come in that night. Didn't even pay attention to that barking dog I assume was yours. Probably barks all the time, right?"

Patrick didn't respond, so Austin continued, "Pretty smart, wasn't I? I even cleaned up any trace of myself with some nice, powerful disinfectant I brought along so none of the dogs would be able to ID me by scent."

"Yeah, smart," Patrick said so disparagingly that Mariah feared Austin would attack him.

But the guy apparently enjoyed describing what he considered to be his brilliance. "Want to know the rest? I'd figured out a great way to corner the world's market for copper and nickel. Other metals, too. Valuable stuff. Some can be sold to utility companies for conducting electricity, some to the government for use in ordnance, whatever. There's already a shortage of lots of metals that are in abundance here, on the sea floor, hidden in manganese nodules. That's pretty complicated, and I don't want to take the time to explain it all to you, but, trust me. Those nodules are worth millions. Billions! I have to do a little blasting, sure, and that doesn't sit well with those glaciers. Big as those suckers are, they're fairly fragile, full of cracks these days. I didn't cause that, so their coming apart isn't really my fault. So, you happy now, Worley? You've got your answers."

"Yeah, I got my answers. You're ruining your competitors by blowing up their mines, and extracting valuable minerals yourself by destroying what nature took millennia to form in this area. You're one fine, upstanding citizen, DeLisio."

"Who cares, as long as I get away with it." He grinned again. "Too bad you won't be around to find out how easy it is for me to weep and wail over what's happening to my friends, while I rake in all that money. In fact, we'll work it out so you and your lady friend, here, get to view one of those glacier breaks firsthand—again—just before you're tossed into the ice-cold water and drown. Assuming you're not crushed on the way down, of course. So sad—this time. I know you helped her escape before, twice. I was watching all visitors up there on the glaciers during the daytime. Knew who was there and when. Why do you think the timing was so perfect?"

Mariah squirmed. She'd gone through too many close calls like that to believe she would survive another one, especially now, when Austin was ready to kill them anyway. But what could Patrick and she do?

She knew one thing she'd love to try. If she could somehow help Patrick shift into wolf form, he'd at least be able to run away, get help.

Too late for her? Most likely. But it might save many more lives—and give Austin DeLisio and his apparent lover Carrie the possibility of being prosecuted for their crimes.

But how could she do that?

For one thing, she could keep Austin bragging and not acting. "I still don't understand how you've been able to mine those—what are they?—undersea manganese nodules without detection. How do you get to them?"

"Oh, now I've got the reporter curious?"

Mariah didn't attempt to correct him by reminding him that she was a nature writer now. Even so, she'd love to thrill her boss Harold and write a genuine tell-all news story about this—assuming they survived.

"It's like this, Mariah. The manganese nodules filled with all those sexy metals were formed by ancient volcanic eruptions. These volcanoes are dormant now, but I cause my own nonvolcanic eruptions by blowing up the ocean floor. The explosions are noisy, and I mask them as much as I can by broadcasting other decoy sounds, like orca calls. I'm sure that excited a nature enthusiast like you, didn't it?"

"And you used the submersible Emil leased to do that?" She aimed a glance at the glaciologist. Emil was clearly enraged, but Carrie kept him still, near the far side of the room, by hanging on to his arm.

"Well, sure. In fact, that's why I told Carrie to have him rent one. He thought his darling daughter was just getting even more enthused about his work here and offering helpful suggestions." By now, DeLisio looked almost relaxed, his legs crossed as he leaned against the kitchen table, the gun no longer aimed directly at Patrick or her.

Could she do anything to give Patrick the time and space he needed?

"You bastard!" Emil said. "And Carrie—I don't believe he talked you into all this." He tried to yank his arm away from his daughter, but she held on.

"You just don't understand, Dad. Austin and I—well, he's really special. You'll see, once you get to know him."

"And you know him? I mean really know him? You're married, Carrie, and Jeremy's a good man. How could you do this to him—let alone fooling me this way? That damned little submarine hasn't been of much use to me at all, and now I learn exactly why you talked me into it. This is terrible, Carrie. I don't understand, but at least I can make things right, even if I can't talk some sense into you. Can I?" Emil's stricken face, already even more drawn than normal, lightened just a little.

"You still don't get it, Dad." Carrie's voice sounded sad. "This is for the future—ours and our country's. You'll see."

Patrick snorted. "So you've deluded yourself into thinking there's some patriotism involved here? Get real, Carrie."

"Oh, she is," Austin said. "It's her father who's out of sync with reality. But he'll get it soon. Right, Emil?"

The chill in Austin's voice caused Emil to look toward him and grow pale. "Are you threatening me?" he asked softly.

"Smart man," Austin said.

"What are you talking about?" Carrie demanded. "You won't hurt my father, will you, Austin?"

"Of course not, darling," he responded. But there was nothing convincing in his tone, even as he put an arm out. Carrie left her father's side in response to the invitation, and Austin pulled her close. But now Emil, too, was a potential target, if Austin decided to start pulling the trigger on his gun.

Mariah glanced at Patrick. He understood, too. But would this latest threat mean they could recruit

Emil, and possibly his daughter, to help them out of this mess?

Or did it just give Austin more impetus to kill Patrick and her right away to relieve himself of the further complication they presented?

She needed to act. Fast.

And was pleased as an idea began to germinate.

Chapter 15

Patrick's fingers twitched as his hands felt permanently set into fists—useless appendages for the moment. He couldn't get close enough to slug DeLisio without putting Mariah in danger of being shot.

He glanced longingly across the room toward where his backpack still lay abandoned near the door. They'd gone through it already, found his 9 mm semiautomatic and his cell phone, but hadn't extracted anything else. Mustn't have figured there was anything important left. If only…

A sound came from beside him. He looked over to find Mariah gasping for breath. "Patrick. I'm

feeling awful. I need my medicine. In your bag…
Please hurry, or I'm going to be sick."

"What's wrong with her?" DeLisio growled.

"She's had some kind of rare stomach ailment,"
Patrick improvised. He knew what Mariah was
doing. Could she pull it off—and get them what they
needed to resolve this situation the right way? "I don't
know the name, but it's sometimes aggravated by
her nerves. If she doesn't get her medicine, she'll
throw up all over the place. Not a pretty sight." Too
weird. He knew it. And too bizarre for a smart guy
to believe. But it was the best he could come up with
in an instant.

And in support of what he'd said, Mariah started
gagging beside him. Smart.

"Look, let me get her medicine from my bag. You
got a glass of water? And is the bathroom through
there?" He pointed toward the door where he'd
assumed there could be another bedroom.

"Stay there!" DeLisio ordered.

"Oh, come on, Austin," Carrie said, her expression
full of disgust. "I don't want to see her puke all over.
Or smell it, even if you make them clean it. I'll keep
an eye on them."

"Fine. Here, take this." He handed her a familiar
pistol: Patrick's semiautomatic. In some ways a good
thing. Patrick was certain his ammo didn't include

silver bullets—although he still doubted that the other firearm had any, either.

But they'd have to act fast. And carefully, to ensure that Mariah didn't get hurt. He hurried across the room, grabbed his knapsack and felt it from the outside to confirm they hadn't taken out any necessities when he was distracted. No, there were the bottle and the light.

He returned for Mariah, whose coughing and choking sounded convincingly real. Putting an arm around her, he led her slowly toward the door. He opened it, pushing it into the bedroom in front of him, and let her go inside first. And then, as Carrie stepped up behind him, the gun at his back, he let himself appear to trip—and fell backward, pushing Carrie away. He grabbed the door and slammed it shut behind him.

Would it lock?

No, but Mariah was already sliding a bulky, heavy easy chair toward him. He helped her use it to prop the door closed.

"What are you doing?" Carrie screamed. "Come out of there." Patrick half expected her to start firing through the closed door, but she didn't. Not yet.

He juggled the chair against the door. It should do the job and ensure the door stayed shut for now.

"There isn't another door out of there," DeLisio yelled, "and we'll be watching the windows."

Which presented another problem. Patrick could maneuver much better in wolf form, had a lot more options for both escaping and attacking, but not if he remained trapped in here.

Quickly, he looked around. There were two windows in this room, and one of frosted glass in the tiny adjoining bathroom.

"If you two don't come out of there soon, I'll use one of my sweet little explosives on this place with you in it. Or maybe I'll just burn it down and not waste anything I can use more productively. Oh, and for the short time you remain alive, you'll have Jeremy's and Emil's deaths on your consciences, too. I won't want them getting in my way."

"What are you talking about?" Carrie's voice was even shriller now. "You can't kill my dad. And I'll simply divorce Jeremy so we can be together. I never wanted him hurt."

"Keep your mouth shut, babe. You know we're a team, and we'll stay that way as long as you play the game on my terms."

"Now's our chance," Patrick whispered. "While they're arguing, they'll be more distracted. I'll change now, get out one of the windows while they're not looking, and circle back to take them down. They'll be watching for a man, not a wolf." The plan sounded good. Now, if only it would work.

Mariah didn't waste any time arguing about the big

picture with him. She dug into his bag and brought out the large bottle of elixir. "Drink some while I get the light." Her eyes were on his, her expression fully confident and even admiring. "Wish I could join you."

"You'll have my back," he assured her. "And I'll have yours."

Quickly, she gave him a brief, hot kiss. "Go to it, wolfman."

"You got it. And you'll get more later." He refused to even think about what else could happen. He opened the container and, without measuring, took a swig even as Mariah pulled out the battery-powered light from the backpack. While he stripped off his human clothing, she switched on the light and held it toward him.

And took in a good, healthy look at his naked body. Too bad they couldn't do anything with it now.

In moments, he felt the change begin—the pulling and stretching of some bones and muscles and internal organs, the shrinking of others.

He felt Mariah's hand on his morphing shoulder. "Patrick…" she said tentatively.

"I'm…fine…" he said before the structure of his mouth elongated and he could speak no more.

Mariah watched Patrick's shifting this time with both anticipation and worry. Of course she appreciated his fine masculine body while he was all man.

She had also come to love his transition, and he had sworn that, despite some discomfort, he relished the change, too.

But was it the right thing for him to do now? What could his wolf form do that his human form could not?

At least he was doing the unexpected. These people couldn't know who Patrick really was, and that his purpose here was as part of the covert military organization known as Alpha Force.

He moaned again, the sound now eerily inhuman. His limbs were no longer straight and strong human arms and legs, but the irregular, furred appendages of a canine. A silver husky-like pelt was erupting all over his skin, and tall, alert ears appeared on the upper sides of his head.

But now what?

"What the hell is he doing?" The shout came from outside the cabin, and Mariah looked up to see Austin DeLisio staring in from the farthest window. "How the hell did Worley— Where is Worley? That dog… What the hell is going on?"

He aimed the gun at the still-closed window and Mariah shrank back against the nearest wall.

"Patrick, get out of his line of sight," she commanded. But would the wolf obey?

She couldn't tell. The wolf who was Patrick stood on all four legs, shook himself, then looked at Mariah. His head then turned until he faced the other window in the room.

The message was obvious, but what would happen if she could get that window open before DeLisio broke the other one? She made her way there quickly, her back still against the wall, and threw the window open.

There was a sharp gun retort and the shattering of glass from across the room as Patrick soared gracefully out the window.

He was free!

Yet not free. There was work to be done. A human to subdue...before he could hurt anyone.

Before he could hurt Mariah.

It was dark outside, but the human—DeLisio— was trying to get back in, to Mariah, through the broken window.

He could not allow that.

Crouching, he stalked his prey swiftly. And then he growled.

DeLisio was partway through the opening. He looked down. And cried out, "What are you?" He aimed the gun he held at Patrick.

And fired.

The shot went through him. Pain...yes.

But no real harm done.
And then Patrick sprang.

Austin had disappeared from the window.

Mariah heard a growl outside, the sound of a fight.

She started toward the window to look out—but then saw that the large chair holding the door closed was moving. The door was opening.

She hurried that way, ready to push the chair again and wedge the door shut. Too late.

Carrie's arm was already inside the room, brandishing another gun—possibly Patrick's, the one they had removed from his backpack. She shot indiscriminately. Fortunately, it missed Mariah.

With no hesitation, Mariah continued forward and closed the door on Carrie's hand. The woman screamed, and Mariah kept increasing the pressure until Carrie dropped the gun.

Lifting the weapon herself, Mariah threw open the door, aiming the gun toward the woman who had wanted to use it on her.

"Stay back, Carrie," she insisted. She glared at Emil, but the older man hadn't moved from the far side of the room where he had been as Patrick and she escaped. And Jeremy remained on the floor.

"Okay, now, you all can just stay here. I'm leaving." She hoped. She wasn't certain what was happening outside, but if all was going as they had planned, Patrick should have Austin under his control. Better yet, unconscious. She would attempt to go out, retrieve his gun and leave—then call the cops to come and clean up. She would let Patrick escape into the woods until he could change again.

Only Carrie clearly didn't intend to cooperate with that. "You bitch!" she screamed. "Where's Austin? Where's Patrick?"

"I think they're having a little altercation outside," Mariah replied—just as Carrie rushed her. Mariah aimed the gun toward her but couldn't bring herself to shoot it.

"You're mine to deal with," Carrie said. "Austin can take care of your damned musher."

Mariah doubted it, but she didn't contradict Carrie, who suddenly grabbed her by the throat. Mariah attempted to hit her with the gun, but that only infuriated the woman even more.

"Carrie, stop it." Emil rushed forward from his position at the far side of the room. But as Mariah let herself go limp to get the pressure off her throat, Carrie grabbed her gun hand.

The gun went off—and Emil fell to the floor.

"Dad! No! You killed him, you bitch!"

"We've got to help him," Mariah shouted, then rammed her head into Carrie's gut. The other woman toppled over, but she still held Mariah's hand. The gun wavered in the air. Instead of helping her father, Carrie kept trying to wrest the gun from Mariah.

"Let go, let go, let go," she shouted—until the outer door opened, and she called, "Austin, help me!"

It wasn't Austin DeLisio who appeared there, but a large, silver wolf, who growled and leaped across the floor toward the fray.

"Where the hell did that come from?" Carrie shouted. Only then did her husband, Jeremy, begin to moan and stir on the floor across the room.

The canine sprang at Carrie, and his teeth were around her wrist. Only when Mariah had taken the gun and scooted several feet away did Patrick let go.

"Thanks," Mariah said to him in relief. "I'll steal back my cell phone, call 9-1-1 and see if we can get some help for Emil. If you can stay just long enough for me to tie Carrie up, that would be great."

The gorgeous golden wolf eyes met hers, and Mariah felt her heart soar.

She had always loved wild animals—and there were none wilder, or more beloved, than the one across the room who had helped to save her life.

Chapter 16

When Mariah heard a car pull up outside only a minute later, she was amazed that help had arrived so fast. But it wasn't EMTs or local law enforcement who came to the front of the cabin and knocked on the door.

The man who stood there was in a military uniform—pale green camouflage fatigues. He was moderate in height, with a nearly shaved head and intense brown eyes.

"Ma'am, I'm Staff Sergeant Jonathon Duvale. I'm looking for a civilian, name of Patrick Worley."

Mariah felt herself begin to relax, if only a little. This could be the person Patrick was told to expect here by his superior officer, an aide being sent from his home base of Ft. Lukman, according to his phone call with Major Drew Connell while they were in the car. If so, this soldier would know who Patrick was. He could be of tremendous assistance right now.

If not—well, she had to find out.

She walked outside and shut the door behind her. From the headlights she could see that the vehicle she'd heard was a military jeep, and there were a couple of other soldiers in it. "Patrick isn't available at the moment, Sergeant. I'm a friend of his, Mariah Garver."

His eyes lit momentarily in apparent recognition of her name. "Then you might know the particulars of my mission here, Ms. Garver...?"

"Could be. Are you a member of Alpha Force?"

"Sure am. Although..."

"I get it." He didn't have to say any more. Mariah figured, from his hesitation, that he was one of the backup guys, and not a shapeshifter like Patrick. "Please call me Mariah. I'm really glad you're here." She gave him a quick rundown on what had happened. "I haven't gone around back," she said quietly, "but my assumption is that Austin DeLisio's body is there. I doubt that he's still alive, and if he's gone, his death could cause a lot of questions—bite marks and all."

"We'll handle it, Mariah." He looked across the

yard toward the dock area where the small submarine was mounted on the pontoon boat. "I suspect that when his body is found in the bay in a few days it'll be hard to tell what happened to him."

"I see," Mariah said.

"And Patrick? He's not here at the moment, is he?"

"No, he…went to get help."

"I figured. Okay, we'd better get busy before the local guys arrive. See you around one of these days, Mariah."

She went back inside, not wanting to watch what these soldiers were up to. In a minute, she heard their vehicle drive away—and not at all too soon, since the local cops got there only a few minutes later.

She hoped that Patrick was far enough away to be safe, but close enough to be aware that help had arrived.

Three days later, Mariah sat in the business center at her B and B going over all her wildlife photographs, after uploading them onto *Alaskan Nature Magazine*'s employee website.

She had some wonderful pictures, definitely enough for an interesting article on the animals in and around Tagoga. Her story wouldn't contain some big revelation about how the decimation of the local glaciers affected the creatures' populations, but that was fine with her. It would be centered more around the kinds of animals she had seen while on the glaciers, primarily on dogsled rides—animals that appeared to thrive on the cold and ice.

She had complimented the Great Glaciers Dogsled Ranch, which she knew would please Toby Dawes. He had hinted at the possibility earlier, when she had initially asked to hire a sled.

She'd also included Tagoga Bay sea life. Not fish killed by the glacier decimation, though. Only the few whales she had actually seen, and dolphins, otters and sea lions.

On the other hand, she was also writing another article that her editor, Harold, would adore—assuming she got the approval to finish it. And she wouldn't finish it, or allow it to be published, without Patrick's, and his superior officers', okay.

Mariah was surprised that what had happened in Emil Charteris's cabin, and the effects on the people there, had quickly taken a different twist from what she had discussed with Sergeant Duvale.

The local media had only gotten snippets of what had allegedly occurred, so there was a lot of buzz around but no real explanation.

That would be up to her—despite lots of irritated contacts from Flynn Shulster, who reminded her that he'd wanted to interview her on his TV show even before she'd had her confrontation with Emil and his family and figured out what really was causing the glacier destruction. He'd offered to pay her well. And give her great publicity for her articles, her boss's publications, whatever.

She had declined as graciously, and firmly, as she could.

Not that she declined *all* publicity, but what she wanted to do was to write about it in a way that was okay with Patrick and his people.

On Patrick's request, she had already sent a story draft to be approved by the officer in charge of Alpha Force, General Greg Yarrow. Once he okayed it, it would become the definitive explanation. And Mariah would have the scoop. Which years ago would have made her gloriously happy. Should even have made her pretty excited now, but she couldn't quite get up the appropriate enthusiasm.

At least it contained the government spin on what allegedly had been happening regarding both the mines in the lower forty-eight and the disappearing glaciers here.

The official story? The now-deceased business mogul Austin DeLisio was involved in both situations. Unfortunately, he would not be able to answer for his alleged misdeeds because he had been killed in Tagoga Bay when the explosives he was about to set—from the submersible his friend Emil

Charteris had inadvertently rented for his nefarious schemes—went off on their own.

He had supposedly been out on a glacier at the time, and his body had been found a day later.

Interesting that Thea Fiske's superstition had apparently come true. There had been a second death, after the second silence in Fiske's Hangout.

"Hello, Mariah."

The door to the business center had opened while her mind wandered, so she hadn't even seen Patrick come in. But now her vision was filled with the wonderful sight of him. His dog, Duke, trotted in at his feet.

"Patrick!" She stood and hurried toward him and into his arms. They hadn't seen much of each other over the past couple of days—although she had confirmed, when he had returned to town a few hours after leaving the cabin, that she had seen the sergeant from Alpha Force. Apparently, Patrick had already been in contact with him and they had coordinated their stories about what had happened to Austin DeLisio.

Mariah reveled in the feel of being held tightly against Patrick. His mouth captured hers in an exquisitely delightful kiss. But thereafter, he broke away.

"Any word from the general about your story?" He was all business again. Just as well. Mariah had already started the process of mentally leaving him, since the physical separation would start much too soon.

"Not yet. Have the cops told you anything about their investigation of DeLisio's 'accident'?"

She sat back down at the computer and began absently to stroke Duke's head.

Both Patrick and she had been debriefed almost immediately by the local authorities, the same ones who had investigated Shaun Bethune's death, including the cop named Pilke, and Detective Gray.

Mariah had truthfully related that Austin DeLisio had admitted killing Shaun because of his expertise in computer research. Shaun had apparently connected the nerdy Fiske's Hangout piano player with the powerful mining magnate and was asking enough questions to make DeLisio nervous. DeLisio had broken into the mushers' building at the Great Glaciers Dogsled Ranch and murdered Shaun.

And then he had collaborated with Carrie Thaxton to get Mariah and Patrick to Emil Charteris's camp to ensure that they wouldn't reveal the truth about him, assuming they knew it. He had left them there, with Carrie holding a gun on them, when he went outside the cabin and presumably departed the site. Fortunately, they'd been able to subdue Carrie.

Jeremy Thaxton was still in the hospital, but was

expected to be okay. Emil's wounds were fairly significant, but he, too, would probably survive.

As would Carrie. But she was under sedation and psychological evaluation. She had admitted to being Austin's lover, to conspiring with him to conduct his dangerous mining operations that had threatened the entire ecological balance here in Tagoga.

All of that had apparently made sense to the local authorities, and to the FBI guys who had also come to debrief her about DeLisio and his operations.

The thing was, she kept raving about werewolves attacking Austin. Coming inside to have conversations with Mariah. Carrie claimed it had something to do with Patrick Worley, but Patrick had been completely accessible to the authorities and cooperated fully in answering their questions. Shapeshifting? Not that Carrie had actually seen anything like that.

Jeremy had been unconscious throughout the ordeal. Emil had been in the other room—and also unconscious, after being shot. Neither of them had seen anything, either. And Patrick had simply laughed at the whole idea, just as the detectives did.

Fortunately, the next full moon was a couple of weeks away. And although Patrick had been shot, since the bullet had not been silver it had caused no harm. He had shown Mariah the nearly healed entry and exit wounds.

"It sounds as if you've accomplished your mission

here," Mariah said brightly. "How long will you stay around?"

"Long enough not to appear suspicious. Turns out there are guys training dogs for the Iditarod near Anchorage that need some extra help, and I'll head that way for a while as part of my cover. From there, I'll continue to Ft. Lukman."

"Right. And I'll be returning to Juneau in another day or two." She bent over and gave Duke a big hug, and the large shepherd-wolfhound mix licked her face. She squeezed her eyes closed to prevent them from tearing up. She would miss this dog. And she would miss his owner even more. She now knew that Patrick's persona as an itinerant musher, with no roots or ambitions, was not really him. That was the kind of man she had learned to run from.

But the man who he really was—a military guy? That held some appeal, might even be worth considering a move away from Alaska someday.

But a military man with secrets like his…how could she ever imagine building a life with him?

Not that he'd even hinted at such a thing.

Her cell phone rang. The number on the caller ID was unfamiliar. "Hello?"

"Ms. Garver, this is General Greg Yarrow."

"Oh, yes, General. I'm with Patrick Worley right now. I'll put you on the speaker phone." She pulled her cell phone away from her ear and pressed the button, noting that Patrick checked to ensure that the business center door was closed. "What did you think about my story of what's been going on around here?"

"Excellent job, Ms. Garver. I can see why Patrick wanted your security clearance given priority, and why he trusted you. You have my approval to send the article to your editor and have it published as is. On behalf of the U.S. government, and most particularly Alpha Force, you have our gratitude for being so understanding about the delicacy of the situation, especially in light of national security and our need for discretion."

She couldn't help beaming, especially at the warm smile Patrick sent her way. "Thank you, General."

"Thanks, Greg," Patrick echoed.

When Mariah hung up, she looked at Patrick. "Well, I guess this is the end of our working together here."

"Yes, but, Mariah, I don't want this to be goodbye."

She shrugged one shoulder, attempting to appear indifferent. "I don't especially, either, but what do you suggest?"

"I don't suppose you'd like to move to the lower forty-eight and write about wildlife around Maryland?"

Mariah had sworn off thinking about serious

relationships with any man a long time ago. And yet, with all that had happened between them, she'd been thinking about what it would be like to spend forever with Patrick—the pros and cons.

But his invitation, though it sounded sincere, didn't suggest forever. Even if it had, she wasn't sure what she would decide. As much as it hurt, she aimed a sardonic smile at him. "Not currently on my agenda. And you? Any thoughts of giving up Alpha Force and staying a part-time dog musher?"

Not that she'd changed her mind about guys with no direction, but at least that might be a way for him to hang out in Alaska—near her.

"Definitely not on my agenda."

"Then I'll see you around, Patrick."

She hoped. Oh, did she hope…but she knew reality was not on their side.

The next few weeks passed quickly—except that time seemed to drag between the communications Mariah received from Patrick. Not that they were sparse. In fact, she received several emails and text messages every day, as well as at least one phone call. None contained any pressure, but there was always an invitation for her to come see him, since after a week in Anchorage he had gone back to Maryland. And a suggestion he would come and see her as soon as he got some leave—if she wanted him to.

She left that door open. And she missed him. A lot. Even though figuring out what to do about it seemed an iffy enterprise at best. And forgetting him seemed impossible, even if the communications stopped— and she absolutely dreaded that possibility.

At least Mariah kept busy—traveling back to Juneau, enjoying the publication of her glacier wildlife article and delighting Harold with her story on Austin DeLisio—including his alleged part in the murder of Shaun Bethune, the havoc wreaked on mines in the lower forty-eight and the damage to the Alaskan glaciers.

She also had to field interview requests by other media folks. She granted only a couple, and those were only after approval by General Yarrow and Patrick. One even included, after all, a short on-air debriefing with Flynn Shulster—to get the persistent pseudoscientist off her back. In all, she was cautious to explain her role as a distant observer who happened to be there when DeLisio was trying to ensure that no one around him was able to voice their suspicions.

About Patrick, she said little—only that she had been helped by a local dog musher whom she had hired a couple of times to take her to visit the glaciers and their wild inhabitants.

Both Emil and Jeremy also gave few interviews, and their responses tended to be circumspect—that they had gone to Alaska strictly to research glaciers and wildlife, and had been totally unaware of who the ostensible piano player at the local bar actually was.

Then there was Carrie Thaxton. She kept screaming about her alleged experiences and what she claimed to have seen, like werewolves, of all things. Her interviewers tended to gently poke fun at her, although stories about her appeared in more than one tabloid newspaper and website, and on Flynn Shulster's show. But she hedged when it came to discussing her relationship with Austin DeLisio, and the reason he had come to Alaska. She had criminal assault charges pending, and her husband and she had separated.

Mariah thought about all of this often—and with special intensity today, as she drove from the hotel where she had booked a room, on Maryland's Eastern Shore, toward the town of Mary Glen.

She had talked Harold into letting her research an article for *Alaskan Nature Magazine* that would compare and contrast the winter wildlife around the Chesapeake Bay with that found in the state she now called home. A bit contrived? Probably, but at least it gave her a reason to be here.

There it was—the small town of Mary Glen. It happened to be the closest town to Ft. Lukman, where Alpha Force was headquartered.

It was also where Dr. Melanie Harding-Connell

maintained her veterinary practice. Mariah had learned from Patrick that Melanie was married to his commanding officer, Major Drew Connell.

And she had inferred that Drew, like Patrick, was one of Alpha Force's shapeshifters.

Mariah had called Melanie and requested a few minutes of her time to interview her as an expert on animals in the area for her article. And if she happened to work in a few questions about what it was like to be married to a werewolf—well, that might be a little awkward without identifying how she knew about Alpha Force. And she had promised General Yarrow to be circumspect about who she talked to and what she said.

Mariah drove her rental car down the main street, Mary Glen Road, until she reached Choptank Lane. She turned and passed the antique shops Melanie had described. The veterinary clinic was one of the two buildings on the second block.

Mariah introduced herself to the receptionist and said she had a meeting scheduled with Dr. Harding-Connell. She was soon shown into the vet's small, well-organized office—and gasped as Melanie held out her hand to greet her. Dr. Melanie Harding-Connell was an attractive woman with deep brown hair and brilliant blue eyes. She wore a white lab jacket—and was clearly pregnant.

"How did you—I mean, under the circumstances,

having a baby… Oh, hell, I'd better stop blabbering."

Melanie laughed as she waved Mariah to a seat facing her desk. "I've heard a lot about you from Patrick," she said. "The guy's definitely smitten with you."

"I—well, I guess I'm smitten with him, too," Mariah admitted. "In a way, that's why I'm here. But…er, I promised General Yarrow to keep my mouth shut about what I know about Alpha Force, but I suspect you know it even better than I do."

Melanie laughed again. "You could say that. And in case you're wondering, this baby is planned. Many of the…more unusual members of Alpha Force pair up with regular people." She came around her desk and sat down on a chair beside Mariah. "Before you decide what to do about Patrick," she said in a low voice, "you need to know that the shapeshifting gene is dominant. I love the idea, but other people might run away screaming." She looked deeply into Mariah's eyes, then smiled. "I suspect you're not one of those."

"I suspect I'm not, too. But this is still a lot to think about." She glanced down at Melanie's protruding belly.

"And marvel at." Melanie took Mariah's hand and put it on her stomach over her lab jacket. Mariah immediately felt movement and gasped in delight.

"That's wonderful."

"Yes," Melanie said, "it is. And I hope to see more of you around here, Mariah. Oh, and if you have any questions about local wildlife, just ask—although you'll forgive me if I keep my answers centered around creatures not associated with Ft. Lukman."

"Absolutely."

A short while later, after Mariah had asked her questions and recorded the interview with Dr. Melanie Harding-Connell, she thanked the vet profusely. "And you like living in the Mary Glen area?"

"I love it here. But of course I chose to move here even before I met Drew. I suspect a writer like you can elect to live anywhere, so hopefully that won't be a factor in your decision."

Assuming she even had a decision to make, Mariah thought a little while later after saying goodbye to the vet.

Heck, she could press the issue if she wanted. And she thought she knew what the answer would be. There was something special between Patrick and her. Something she had felt the very first time she had seen him...as a person. Something that had continued when she had glimpsed him in wolf form, as well.

She used her global positioning system, as well as the directions Melanie had given her, to drive along the remote roads through the woods toward

Ft. Lukman. She hadn't told Patrick she was coming, but had confirmed in their most recent communications that he was in town.

Her cell phone rang. It was Patrick. She used her hands-free gadget to answer. "Hi, Patrick," she said.

"Okay, Mariah," he began, "this is kind of out of the blue, but I can't stand how things are between us now."

Her heart sank. Had she come all this way to have him dump her without even knowing she was nearby?

"So here's how it is. I'm working on getting a permanent assignment to one of the Alaskan military bases—maybe Fort Wainwright in Fairbanks. I'll probably need to do a lot of traveling, but at least we'll be closer together. And maybe you could move to Fairbanks from Juneau. But I really want to give this a try, and hope you'll at least consider it."

Mariah saw the gate that led into Ft. Lukman. "Well…" She drew the word out, letting him worry for a short while. "On the other hand, I rather like the area around Mary Glen. And if you'll tell the sentry on duty at your front gate to let me come in, I'll tell you in person just how much—"

"You're here? Hell, yes, I'll tell him. Wait in the parking area just inside the gate."

The guard let Mariah in, and she did as Patrick said.

In less than five minutes he came running up the road that apparently led to the rest of the military base. He was dressed in camouflage fatigues and looked more like a soldier than she had ever seen him—and sexier than ever.

Or maybe that was because of their separation.

In moments, she was in his arms. His kisses were hot and welcoming and definitely suggestive.

"You're here," he said when he finally pulled back just enough to speak. His light brown eyes were soft and loving, and Mariah felt she could get lost in them. Forever.

"Yes, I'm here, wolfman," she whispered. "And I'm here to stay."

* * * * *

HARLEQUIN®

n o c t u r n e ™

COMING NEXT MONTH

Available December 28, 2010

HARLEQUIN®

A Romance

FOR EVERY MOOD™

Spotlight on
Classic

Quintessential, modern love stories
that are romance at its finest.

See the next page
to enjoy a sneak peek from
the Harlequin Presents® series.

Harlequin Presents® is thrilled
to introduce the first installment of
an epic tale of passion and drama by
USA TODAY *Bestselling Author*
Penny Jordan!

*When buttoned-up Giselle first meets
the devastatingly handsome Saul Parenti,
the heat between them is explosive....*

"LET ME GET THIS STRAIGHT. Are you actually suggesting that I would stoop to that kind of game playing?"

Saul came out from behind his desk and walked toward her. Giselle could smell his hot male scent and it was making her dizzy, igniting a low, dull, pulsing ache that was taking over her whole body.

Giselle defended her suspicions. "You don't want me here."

"No," Saul agreed, "I don't."

And then he did what he had sworn he would not do, cursing himself beneath his breath as he reached for her, pulling her fiercely into his arms and kissing her with all the pent-up fury she had aroused in him from the moment he had first seen her.

Giselle certainly *wanted* to resist him. But the hand she raised to push him away developed a will of its own and was sliding along his bare arm beneath the sleeve of his shirt, and the body that should have been arching away from him was instead melting into him.

Beneath the pressure of his kiss he could feel and taste her gasp of undeniable response to him. He wanted to devour her, take her and drive them both until they were equally satiated—even whilst the anger within him that she should make him feel that way roared and burned its resentment of his need.

She was helpless, Giselle recognized, totally unable to withstand the storm lashing at her, able only to cling to the man who was the cause of it and pray that she would survive.

Somewhere else in the building a door banged. The sound exploded into the sensual tension that had enclosed them, driving them apart. Saul's chest was rising and falling as he fought for control; Giselle's whole body was trembling.

Without a word she turned and ran.

Find out what happens when Saul and Giselle succumb to their irresistible desire in

THE RELUCTANT SURRENDER

Available January 2011 from Harlequin Presents®

REQUEST YOUR
FREE BOOKS!
2 FREE NOVELS PLUS 2 FREE GIFTS!

HARLEQUIN®

nocturne™

Dramatic and Sensual Tales of Paranormal Romance.

YES! Please send me 2 FREE Harlequin® Nocturne™ novels and my 2 FREE gifts (gifts are worth about $10). After receiving them, if I don't wish to receive any more books, I can return the shipping statement marked "cancel." If I don't cancel, I will receive 4 brand-new novels every other month and be billed just $4.47 per book in the U.S. or $4.99 per book in Canada. That's a saving of at least 15% off the cover price! It's quite a bargain! Shipping and handling is just 50¢ per book.* I understand that accepting the 2 free books and gifts places me under no obligation to buy anything. I can always return a shipment and cancel at any time. Even if I never buy another book from Harlequin, the two free books and gifts are mine to keep forever.

238/338 HDN E9M2

Name
(PLEASE PRINT)

Address
Apt. #

City
State/Prov.
Zip/Postal Code

Signature (if under 18, a parent or guardian must sign)

Mail to the **Reader Service:**
IN U.S.A.: P.O. Box 1867, Buffalo, NY 14240-1867
IN CANADA: P.O. Box 609, Fort Erie, Ontario L2A 5X3
Not valid for current subscribers to Harlequin Nocturne books.

Want to try two free books from another line?
Call 1-800-873-8635 or visit www.ReaderService.com.

* Terms and prices subject to change without notice. Prices do not include applicable taxes. N.Y. residents add applicable sales tax. Canadian residents will be charged applicable provincial taxes and GST. Offer not valid in Quebec. This offer is limited to one order per household. All orders subject to approval. Credit or debit balances in a customer's account(s) may be offset by any other outstanding balance owed by or to the customer. Please allow 4 to 6 weeks for delivery. Offer available while quantities last.

Your Privacy: Harlequin Books is committed to protecting your privacy. Our Privacy Policy is available online at www.ReaderService.com or upon request from the Reader Service. From time to time we make our lists of customers available to reputable third parties who may have a product or service of interest to you. If you would prefer we not share your name and address, please check here. ☐

Help us get it right—We strive for accurate, respectful and relevant communications. To clarify or modify your communication preferences, visit us at www.ReaderService.com/consumerchoice.

HN10

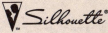

ROMANTIC

SUSPENSE

Sparked by Danger, Fueled by Passion.

NEW YORK TIMES BESTSELLING AUTHOR

RACHEL LEE

No Ordinary Hero

Strange noises...a woman's mysterious disappearance
and a killer on the loose who's too close for comfort.

With no where else to turn, Delia Carmody looks
to her aloof neighbour to help, only to discover
that Mike Windwalker is no ordinary hero.

Available in December.
Wherever books are sold.

Visit Silhouette Books at www.eHarlequin.com

SRS27709R

Silhouette® Desire

HAVE BABY, NEED BILLIONAIRE

MAUREEN CHILD

Simon Bradley is accomplished, successful and very proud. The fact that he has to prove he's fit to be a father to his own child is preposterous. Especially when he has to prove it to Tula Barrons, one of the most scatterbrained women he's ever met. But Simon has a ruthless plan to win Tula over and when passion overrules prudence one night, it opens up the door to an affair that leaves them both staggering. Will this billionaire bachelor learn to love more than his fortune?

Billionaires and Babies

Available January wherever books are sold.

Always Powerful, Passionate and Provocative.

SD73072